When Jesus Came to the Cracker Barrel

When Jesus Came to the
CRACKER BARREL

AND OTHER STORIES

Michael Braswell

RESOURCE *Publications* · Eugene, Oregon

WHEN JESUS CAME TO THE CRACKER BARREL
And Other Stories

Resource Publications
An Imprint of Wipf and Stock Publishers
199 W. 8th Ave., Suite 3
Eugene, OR 97401

www.wipfandstock.com

PAPERBACK ISBN: 979-8-3852-3027-3
HARDCOVER ISBN: 979-8-3852-3028-0
EBOOK ISBN: 979-8-3852-3029-7

Dedicated to my Tuesday morning reunion group

Table of Contents

Acknowledgments

In addition to new stories for this collection, a number of the stories have been previously published in *Morality Stories* (Carolina Academic Press), *Growing Up South of the Mason-Dixon Line* (Wipf and Stock: Resource), *Remembering Peleliu* (Branden Books) and *Stray Dogs* (Second Street Press). It should also be noted that Scott Braswell is the author of "Sarah Salvation" and primary author of "Sunday Biscuits." Special thanks to Roberta Teague Herin and Susan Braswell for reading and making suggestions for this manuscript.

1   *A Small Piece of Blue Sky*

"I have seen things."

That's all Gerald would say to Dr. Breedlove, his VA psychiatrist.

On the 15th of each month, Gerald's parents, Eugene and Eula Smithwick, dutifully drove their son to Asheville for his appointment at the veteran's hospital. After each session, Dr. Breedlove would talk briefly with them about how he was tweaking this or that medication to help improve Gerald's condition. He spoke the right words, but his eyes told a different story. Eugene and Eula would nod their heads and look at each other. They might be country folks, but country folks possessed better bullshit detectors than most city dwellers, so they soon figured out that the VA Doc was more or less clueless about what to do for their son.

Gerald could take care of most of his basic needs, but most of the time he sat on the back porch, looking out toward the mountains. With a little coaxing from Eula, he would eat a bite or two at mealtime. Occasionally, he might comment briefly on a memory, but mostly he would remain silent except when he would whisper, "I have seen things."

Sometimes his wounded mantra would be followed by brief sobs. From the vacant look in his eyes and the frozen expression on his face, it was clear to his parents that what he had seen had stopped him in his tracks and put him in some kind of in-between place that was neither here nor there.

Eugene spoke into McDonald's squawk box. "Two senior coffees, one black, one with cream, and one caramel sundae with nuts."

Eula was a frugal woman except when it came to her son and McDonald's caramel sundaes—sometimes she ordered two at the same time. Eugene shook his head at the thought of it.

Merging with traffic on the four-lane bypass around Burnsville, Eugene pointed his trusty old Buick toward home. He sipped his coffee while Eula polished off her sundae and Gerald sat silently in the back seat.

"We been doing this for almost a year now with almost nothing to show for it. What's the point?" Eugene said as much to himself as to his wife.

Eula looked out the window at the hint of fall's first color. "We do what we can."

"I knew that fourth tour in Iraq was going to get him—I could see it in his eyes. We shouldn't have let him go," Eugene replied with a grimace.

Eula looked at her husband, then glanced at her son in the back seat.

Gerald sat erect with his hands folded in his lap, saying nothing—seeing nothing.

"There were signs," Eugene continued. "He had trouble sleeping on his last leave home— and nightmares. He never had them before Iraq."

Eula sipped her coffee before responding, wondering why her husband didn't tell them to put in two creams in instead of one. "His unit was ordered up. What choice did he—we—have?"

Gripping the steering wheel with both hands, Eugene gave his wife a sideways glance. "There's always a choice."

"Maybe the new medicine will . . ." Eula's voice trailed off.

"Medicine, my ass," Eugene grunted. "Gerald needs something pills can't fix."

"Like what?"

Eugene relaxed his grip on the steering wheel. "Not sure, but I did hear about a healer up on Humpback Mountain. Goes by the name of Lester Simpkins."

"A healer? My Lord, Eugene, you've got to be kidding."

Eugene's brow furrowed. "You got any better ideas?"

Eula folded her arms across her chest. "I feel a migraine coming on."

Three days later, the Buick bucked and rattled its way along the dirt lane that passed for a road in the backwoods of Humpback Mountain.

"I don't have a good feeling about this," Eula observed as Eugene pulled their sedan to a stop in front of a small, ramshackle mountain cabin and announced, "This is it."

On the front porch, Lester Simpkins sat on what was left of a church pew. He was a thin stick of a man. His long white beard mixed with a bit of gray moved gently with the breeze. He wore a faded Green Bay Packers sweatshirt over his work pants and an Atlanta Braves baseball cap perched at an angle on his bald head. Lester Simpkins' gray-green eyes followed the three people walking toward him.

Eugene walked ahead and stopped a few feet from the front porch. "Howdy. Are you Mr. Simpkins, the healer?"

"Name's Lester. And who might you be?"

"My name's Eugene and this here is my wife, Eula, and my son, Gerald," Eugene replied. "Some folks down in Bakersville told me how to get here—that you were a healer. Royce Laney down at Kim's Diner called you 'the Jesus Man.'"

"Like I said, Eugene, my name's Lester."

Eugene glanced uneasily at his wife. "Well, Lester, I got to tell you up front, we ain't believers—I mean as Christians and such. We don't go to church except for weddings and funerals. So, to be honest with you, we aren't reliable in the Christianity department."

Lester smiled. "Then you'd probably fit right in with many of my Christian friends. Saint Francis preached to the birds which I expect were a lot more reliable than his human flock."

Lester looked at Gerald. "Looks like your son has a troubled spirit."

3

Gene put his arm around his son's shoulder. "Can you help him?"

"Don't know. Maybe, maybe not, but I can give it a try. Why don't the two of you take a walk down through the apple orchard for an hour or so while me and Gerald get acquainted."

When Gerald's parents disappeared around the barn on their way to the orchard, Lester took off his cap and pulled his chair up close to Gerald's. Sitting knee-to-knee, he took Gerald's hand in his. Lester could feel Gerald tense up at his touch.

"That's alright, son. You've been through a lot. We'll just sit here and rest a spell."

Lester sat with his eyes closed, holding Gerald's hand for the better part of an hour. From time to time, he would exhale a soft, low moan.

Opening his eyes, Lester leaned toward Gerald who offered him a passing glance from the corner of his eye.

"I've seen things."

"Yes, you have, son. Yes, you have," Lester replied, patting the young man's hand. "You've been traveling down the low road of sorrow for some time now. You saw behind a curtain you didn't want to pull back and found yourself buried in the quicksand of regret."

A thin bead of perspiration broke out on Lester's forehead as he continued. "All you see are dark clouds and the unspeakable that's hiding behind them. You feel lost in that dark and fearful place where the light can't get through. Those storm clouds of suffering have carried you away from the memory of the blue sky that remains. I'm going to do my best to help you find a small piece of that blue sky—just enough blue in the middle of the storm that surrounds you to remember how to find your way back. You won't be alone. I'm going to walk with you. Yesiree, me and you are going to do it together."

Lester squeezed Gerald's hand gently. "I'm going to pray myself into the middle of your sadness, so me and you can go a'looking for that piece of blue sky."

Lester placed his right hand on Gerald's heart and his left on the back of Gerald's head. Forehead to forehead, Lester began to pray in a kind of whispering silence. As his intercession for Gerald intensified, he and Gerald began to slowly rock back and forth.

Then Gerald began to cry. A long, piercing moan rose out of him, starting deep down in his gut, snaking its way up through every cell in his body. Opening his mouth, Gerald exhaled a prolonged howl that was more animal than human—a sound like no other Lester had ever heard—a sound that ended in the quiet scream of a baby's cry. Gerald collapsed in Lester's arms.

Eugene and Eula walked hand in hand up the pathway from the orchard. The knots in their stomachs gave testimony to the question that waited for an answer. Rounding the corner of the barn, they saw Lester and Gerald sitting on the front porch sipping coffee. Eula could feel tears welling up in her eyes. Her son was looking at her—seeing her. She squeezed her husband's hand.

When they arrived at the porch, she spoke his name: "Gerald."

Her son looked at his mother and father and said, "I have seen things."

Eugene looked at his wife, then his son. "You have?"

Gerald nodded. "I have seen blue sky."

Eugene wanted to pay Lester for his help, but Lester would have none of it. He tipped his hat to Eugene and said, "A clear, blue sky is the breath of heaven. How could a man worth his salt think of charging someone for a piece of that?"

2 *Seeds of Change*

"Why not, Mother?"

Missy Simerly's complaint was vivid and compelling, colored by an independent streak and the ache of childhood friendship.

"Don't take that tone with me," Eunice Simerly replied as she rubbed Jergens body lotion onto her arms. "You are twelve years old, young lady. Old enough to end your tomboy ways. It's time for you to start acting like a young lady."

Missy balled up her fists in frustration. "Why can't Nellie come play with me like she used to? Why can't Naomi bring her on Saturdays when she comes to do the ironing?"

Eunice pursed her lips. "Your playing days with Nellie are over. Nellie's a good girl and her mother is a good woman, but we live in difficult times. One day you will understand . . . not today, but one day you will . . ." Missy's mother's voice trailed off as the screen door creaked open with Naomi Jones standing there.

"Ironing's done and Sunday's pie is warming on the stove."

"Oh my, Naomi. I didn't realize what time it is. Are you ready for me to drive you home?" Eunice gasped.

"Yessum, I 'spect so," Naomi replied, offering a sideways nod to Missy.

Eunice massaged the last of the lotion into the palms of her hands. "Okie dokie then. And Naomi . . ."

"Yessum?"

"Don't forget to take that leftover chicken from last night's supper home with you."

Naomi fetched her hat and coat from the broom closet. "Yessum. Thank you."

Eunice picked up her purse and car keys from the hallway antique table. "Oh, you are most welcome. The chicken fricassee you prepared is one of Ed's favorites. I trust it will be just as tasty for you and Marvin once it's warmed up."

Missy stood on the front porch and watched her mother's station wagon back out of the driveway with Naomi sitting in the back seat. A thought floated through her consciousness: "back seat of the bus, back seat of the station wagon." She wasn't certain what it meant. There was a sameness to such back seat traditions. It was what she was used to, the way things had always been as far as she knew.

Mose, the yard man looked up from the rose bush he was trimming. "Young'un, you be alright?"

"I guess so, Mose. The world is becoming mighty strange."

Mose loosened up the red kerchief that he wore around his neck and wiped the sweat from his face. "You be okay, child. The Lord will work it all out in his own good time."

Missy Simerly through no fault of her own was caught in the throes of major change. Her best friend, Nellie, was the first Negro girl to integrate the school Missy attended.

She overheard her father tell her mother while reading the latest headlines from the local newspaper, "My dear, the natural order is being challenged." Eunice Simerly reminded her husband that Reverend Ernest Bosco had told her last week after Sunday Services that such change was not Biblical, but was the Devil's temptation. Besides, he had it on good authority that M.L. King, Jr. was a communist.

August Simerly folded the newspaper he had been reading and looked at his wife.

"I wouldn't put too much stock in what Ernie Bosco says. As I recall, last year he claimed to have a visitation by the angel, Gabriel, while fishing on the Flint River.

"Well, he is our preacher," Eunice retorted.

Her husband offered her a wisp of a smile. "That, he is. But it helps to remember that all Reverends aren't created equal."

Eunice pushed her point. "A man of God is a man of God."

August reached for his pipe. "Perhaps, but most men of God I know don't prefer a jigger of Four Roses in their afternoon coffee."

Lighting his pipe, he continued. "All I'm saying is because the order we are accustomed to may be natural to us, doesn't mean it's natural to others."

"You mean, the Negroes?"

"Yep, that's what I mean. In any event, Bob Dylan's right. 'The times, they are a'changing.' And maybe, it's time that they did."

Eunice rose from her chair and smoothed out her skirt. "Well, I can't believe you are listening to the likes of him. Anyway, I heard he was a Communist too."

Her husband laughed. "Is it possible that anyone who doesn't see things your way is a Communist?"

The attic fan pushed the linen curtains, creating a breeze of sorts into Missy's room. Laying on her bed, she thought about Nellie. They had played together since they were five. Once a week, every Saturday, Naomi brought Nellie with her when she came to clean house and cook the evening meal for Missy's family. Once, when Missy's younger brother JT, called Naomi a nigger when she wouldn't let him have another cookie, her father found out about it and gave JT what folks down South referred to as a "whupping." Although she was only 12, Missy possessed a keen sense of observation. She was glad her parents weren't prejudiced like some of the other people she knew, but still . . . there was something going on, she didn't know what, that made her feel uneasy. As she lay there, her mind wandered back to years past and the games she and Nellie played together.

They played everything from hop scotch, to checkers to dolls. Less frequently, they played Missy's favorites, horse shoes and the basketball game of "horse." They were good memories for the most part, but as her memory pulled back more layers, Missy pondered the more subtle, nuanced responses Nellie relied on in their childhood games. While Missy had no doubt their affection for each other was genuine, she had to admit that Nellie almost always played second fiddle to her, deferring to her wishes even when they hinged on the selfish or demanding side of things. Looking closely into her past, Missy came to recognize the polite shadow that fell across Nellie's face when she felt she was being treated unfairly or the slight arch of her eyebrow that signaled some hint of hidden anger even as a practiced smile pursed her lips. Now, Missy saw those same subtle cues and responses each morning Nellie walked the gauntlet past the white students' stares and whispers into the school that didn't want her. Tomorrow would another day at school, a day like most other school days for her, but not for Nellie.

Recess was a welcome break from the monotony of Elvin Elrod's Civics class. Reading from his precisely typed notes with the cadence of a funeral home director, he would occasionally peer over his horn-rimmed glasses and proclaim, "Any questions?" followed immediately by "Well, then," as he continued reading aloud to himself.

Missy, Nancy and Rose Marie were playing "jump rope" when she heard Dickie Lee Jones' whine of a voice state with an air of false bravado, "You ain't welcome around here. You and your kind need to go back to Africa where you belong."

Picking up the jump rope, she walked over to where a small group of ne'er-do-wells had gathered around the picnic table where Nellie was staring at the pages of her Civics book, her shadowed face straining at practiced politeness. Stu Esom giggled nervously, but then Stu was known to giggle from time to time for no reason at all.

Looking around at his audience was a new experience for Dickie Lee, a kind of first-time attention that was focused on him alone. Turning back to Nellie, his whine quickly morphed into his best attempt at a growl. "Did you hear me, Nigger?"

Missy could feel the heat rising in her face. Nancy noted her friend's reddening cheeks and whispered to Rose-Marie, "Uh oh. Fire in the hole. We best step back."

Every kid there, was aware that when provoked, Miss could display a bit of temper. When faced with adverse circumstances, Missy Simerly more often than not, chose fight over flight.

Missy stepped forward. "Dickie Lee Jones, leave Nellie alone, if you know what's good for you."

Dickie looked at the others for some sign of support before turning back to Missy. "What are you, some kind of Nigger lover?"

All eyes shifted from Dickie Lee to Missy, waiting to see what would happen next.

"Nellie Mae Johnson is my friend. If that makes me a Nigger lover, then so be it," Missy replied, her voice rising.

The small assortment of befuddled sixth graders issued forth a collective gasp as their eyes asked the question: Was Missy with them and their parents or did she stand with the unwelcome intruder sitting at the picnic table?

Unsure of what his next move should be, Dickie Lee Jones made the wrong choice. Wanting to cash in on the attention he was getting, he went nose to nose with Missy and spewed forth, "then why don't you go back to Africa with her and her bunch?"

No one present could clearly recollect the order of what happened next. All they could remember was that before Dickie Lee could finish sounding out the last word— "bunch"—for effect, in a split second, Missy Simerly began to whip him with the jump rope she had wrapped around her right hand. She pummeled him with the wooden handles, busting his lip and catching his left eye with a strike that would have made Lash LaRue proud. To make matters worse, in that day, boys weren't supposed to hit girls, which further handicapped Dickie. Stunned by the ferocity of Missy's surprise attack, Dickie Lee Jones went into full retreat mode, running for his life toward the safety of Miss Edna Fogelburg, the recess supervisor. The bloodied sight of Dickie caused Edna to drop the apple she was nibbling on in horror.

After directing Dickie Lee to the school nurse, she huffed and hustled over to the scene of the assault. Snatching the jump rope from Missy's hand, Edna chortled, "Young lady, you are in a world of trouble! Off you go to the principal's office. I will be right behind you."

The befuddled group of sixth graders stared at the unfolding scene in silence. Missy stole a quick glance toward Nellie as she made her way to the administrative office. The shadows disappeared for a fleeting moment before Nellie returned to her book.

Little was said on the ride home from school. Daddy drove and Mother bemoaned the actions of her errant, misguided daughter with a nonverbal guttural expression of "mmm . . . mmm . . ." But once they got inside, the inquisition began.

Missy's father sat down in his chair and folded his hands in his lap while his wife paced to and fro, gesturing with her hands as she spoke.

"Ed Simerly, what are you going to do about our daughter? If this keeps up, she is going to be the death of me. We won't be able to show our face in town or in church. And good lord, of all the children to get into a fracas with, she picks on Dickie Lee Jones whose mother by the way, is President of the Garden Club. I won't be able to look Matilda in the eye though that won't matter, because she will probably never speak to me again!"

Eunice slumped down on the sofa and held her head in her hands, talking as much to herself as to her husband. "I've tried. Lord knows I've tried to raise her to be a lady. I've told her it's time to give up her tomboy habits. No matter what, she continues to defy me and go her own way. I've prayed about it until I'm blue in the face. I don't know what else to do."

Missy stopped the rocking chair. "Dickie Lee was calling Nellie names. He was bullying her, and no one did anything about it. And . . ."

Eunice Simerly interrupted her daughter in mid-sentence. "That's not your concern. You need to stay out of this integration mess."

"But . . .," Missy tried to interject.

"No buts about it," her mother replied. "I should have never let Naomi bring her to play with you in the first place. All it's done is cause trouble and embarrassment."

Missy stared at her balled-up fists, the rhythmic creak of the rocking chair signaling the rising of her temperature.

"Well, Ed, are you going to sit there like a bump on a log or be the man of the house?"

Ed looked at his daughter, then at his wife. "I thought I would let you finish before I spoke. Are you through?"

Eunice looked at Ed with fire in her eyes. "Yes, I am through!"

"Okay then," Ed replied. "As the man of the house I have to say Missy, I am disappointed that you couldn't control your temper. That it resulted in you being sent home."

Eunice pointed at her daughter. "Do you hear that, young lady? Do you hear that?"

Ed cleared his throat. "However, . . . "

Eunice's eyes grew wide. "However, what?"

Casting a warning glance his wife's way, Ed continued. "However, Nellie is your friend and It's not a bad thing to stand up for your friends, preferably without resorting to violence. Fighting and such never really solves anything."

Missy's mother rose from the sofa in a huff and left the room.

Her father's expression softened. "Are you all right, my rambunctious young daughter?"

Missy stopped rocking. "I guess so. I know I'm supposed to be sorry about what I did to Dickie Lee, but you and I both know that I'm not."

Her father stood up from his chair and winked at his daughter. "Sometimes the truth hurts. I bet those jump rope handles left a mark. How about I make us some hot chocolate?"

Missy sensed more than understood that a kind of precarious, sometimes tense balance existed in her home, the balance between her high-strung "what will the neighbors think" mother and her low-keyed discipline with a wink father. Their relationship brought her an uneasy reassurance tinged with the anxiety such a tension engenders. Adding to the mix of confusion and chaos of the world changing beneath her feet, strained a twelve-year-old girl's imagination between what had always been and what was yet to come.

Hunched over on the garden bench lost in thought, Missy didn't notice Mose approaching with his garden hoe.

Mose kneeled down beside her. "Child, what be troublin' you?"

Missy shrugged her shoulders. "Mose, I don't what to make of things anymore. Lately, I can't seem to stay out of trouble."

"No doubt 'bout that," Mose replied with a smile. "Troubles do come our way. Question is, what do we do when they arrive on our doorstep? 'Course, only the Good Lord knows how and when it end."

Missy rubbed her eye. "If it will end. Will it end, Mose?"

"Sure 'nuff, it will. All things pass in time, the good and the bad. You too young to understand, but you different than most folks. You be seed corn."

Missy looked puzzled. "What's seed corn, Mose?"

Mose looked at Missy before speaking. "You be one of the special ones, Miss Missy. The seed corn special like you. All crops depend on it. The people depend on it. If anyone eats the seed corn, folks starve. So, folks protect it. They future depend on it. You and your kind the future. What you see going on now will soon be the past."

Missy placed her hand on Mose's knee. "Sounds nice, but I'm not sure I understand. All I know is that I'm tired. I'm tired of getting into trouble, of upsetting my mother . . . but I can't seem to help it . . . especially the way they treat Nellie at school. Most of the teachers ignore her. Not Mrs. Frazier, our English teacher. She's nice to Nellie. But not the others. And the students, even some of my friends, are worse. They laugh at her and call her names."

Mose rose to his feet and picked up his hoe. "I hear 'bout you and the Jones boy. They say you gave him a sure 'nuff whipping."

Missy shook her head. "When I get mad, sometimes I can't seem to stay put. My parents say I don't have enough self-discipline. Maybe, I don't. But I don't like bullies. When Dickie Lee got on Nellie's case, I told him to stop."

Rolling himself a cigarette, Mose looked at Missy. "And when he didn't?"

"When he didn't, he went nose to nose with me," Missy replied. "I don't like folks getting in my face. I guess that's when I took to the jump rope."

Mose lit his cigarette. "So, how about now, young'un? That be in your past. Tomorrow be a new day. . . can be a good day at school for you."

Missy's countenance turned serious. "That depends."

"Depends on what, Child?"

Missy looked at Mose. "Depends on what happens when I sit with Nellie tomorrow at lunchtime. She shouldn't have to eat alone. Maybe, I'll bring my jump rope with me."

3　*Sarah Salvation*

Like a cockroach seduced by a bug light, Francis Quiet Moon shuffled to the edge of an unmarked street corner and stared into the flickering pulse of a streetlamp. A frayed, mustard-yellow knit cap nearly swallowed his head, and his tired frame ached inside the stained, gas-station-attendant's shirt he was wearing. A tattered American flag was tied around his waist—some of the stars had been filled in by different colored crayons, courtesy of his two sons who lived with their mother. His feet were decorated by red and green bowling shoes two sizes too big.

What was left of his existence was stuffed into his Vietnam-issue duffel bag, Francis had hitchhiked but mostly walked his way through the last 100 miles of hill country, traveling the cracked back of a stubborn two-lane that twisted and curled around the Carolina mountains like a serpent. When he walked, the dog tags around his neck clinked like the teeth of a chattering skull. The sound made Francis uncomfortable and he thought about how something as insignificant as two pieces of metal hitting each other could bring back so many bad memories—before and after the war. At one time, Francis had built wind chimes in the cramped basement of the garage apartment he rented with his wife. He couldn't stand the sound of them anymore. They made his head hurt and his heart ache. At night, he would try to force those memories away, make them set with the sun. But every morning they would rise again, burning into his back as he walked, never letting him forget.

He had been losing his grip on sobriety since dawn and had to concentrate just to keep his balance. Francis cringed as the sounds of a honky-tonk version of Sinatra's "My Way" crackled from a nearby convenience store. Picking at the loose threads of his toboggan, he retrieved a near-empty bottle of "Cisco" brand liquor from beneath the remnants of Old Glory. He would often, as he described it, "Disco with Cisco," referring to the bottle as his faithful friend, "Fran-Cisco." The bottle spilled the truth to Francis in a numbing language he could understand. It never cheated on him, never lied to him, or blamed him for a failed marriage. It never confronted him with his past or promised him a future. Although "Fran-Cisco" had been his best friend since a rehab stint after the war, the relationship was stormy. But at least it was his. At least, he could depend on it.

He closed his eyes, took two quick, punishing gulps and gritted his teeth. Peeling open his left eye to squint, Francis could barely make out the lettering of a neon-crimson sign that spelled *Crystal Grape Diner*. Lured by the aroma of food, he slowly gathered up his road-weary carcass and stumbled across the intersection.

Francis stepped inside the diner and slid into a tattered, lime green booth patched by gray duct tape. Sounds from a Crosby, Stills, Nash & Young forty-five wafted from an elaborate jukebox squatting in a smoky corner of the diner like some kind of mechanized Sumo wrestler. Francis' hollow eyes scanned the surroundings for signs of activity while his fingers fumbled with a half-empty pack of Marlboro Lights. He thought about how he used to never smoke. His wife hated it.

Settling on a cigarette that seemed dry enough to ignite, Francis lit up. Inhaling deeply, he ran his hands through his hair and observed the other examples of aimless humanity around him. An elderly man in a wheelchair, hooked up to an oxygen tank and dressed in a threadbare tuxedo, played solitaire at one booth. He would light a fresh cigarette every few minutes and let it burn on the edge of an ashtray, never smoking it, just letting it burn.

Francis' eyes followed a succession of Elvis paintings to the other side of the room where a small ruckus was erupting.

He extinguished his cigarette on a small tin ashtray and peered through the smoke. A young woman, dressed in a checkered apron and combat boots, was juggling steak sauce bottles, three and four at a time to the cackling delight of four elderly, drunken La-Z-Boy warriors. After finishing her performance, the waitress took a modest bow, laid the party's check on the table, and disappeared into the kitchen. The old men applauded her and were still snorting with laughter as they began to eat their food.

Francis was about to light up another Marlboro when he caught the scent of a pleasant fragrance. A smudged menu slid gently across his knuckles as he lit the cigarette and looked up. Smiling lips asked to take his order. Francis looked above the lips, into eyes warm and dark, shimmering as if fireflies were trapped inside. The tag artfully stitched onto her shirt said "Sarah." She glanced at his duffel bag while fumbling in her pocket for a pen.

"Where ya headed?" she inquired.

"Home," Francis replied in a raspy voice brought on by the late autumn cold.

"Where's home?"

"Don't know yet," he answered, grinning and rubbing his head.

She smiled to herself and nodded while pulling out her pad and pencil to take his order.

"What are your specials tonight?" Francis mumbled.

"Honey, everything I make is special."

Francis drew deeply from his cigarette and grinned so wide his face hurt.

"Well, how about a special cheeseburger and some special fries?"

The woman chuckled while taking down his order.

"You're pretty good with those bottles," he added, putting out another cigarette.

"Oh, yeah," she said, laughing. "Well, the way I see it, everybody has a special talent, and I guess juggling Heinz 57 bottles for the enjoyment of my red-eyed regulars is mine."

"Aren't you afraid of dropping one of those bottles on some-one's head or something?" Francis inquired, rubbing his chapped nose. "You know, with all the lawsuits these days, and what not?"

She smiled and took the menu from his trembling fingers.

"Sometimes you gotta do something risky to make sure you're still alive," she whispered. "Something special, coming up."

She smiled at Francis and clomped off in her combat boots toward the kitchen.

Francis laughed to himself and shook his head in amazement. Taking a last draw from his cigarette, he looked out the window and watched a couple of young boys in the shadows across the street, kicking an old cardboard box around. He wondered what their names were. His head began to hurt.

He wondered what his own boys were doing, what they had for dinner, what they dreamed about. Francis wondered if they wondered about him. Lighting another cigarette, he thought about how his boys used to always be in his dreams. These visions were like mirrors stitched on his heart, reflecting a time long since past. The last dream he had was like something out of a movie. It involved a big spread of blue sky that looked like a movie screen in the middle of a dark space. One arm, with the palm open, came in from one side of the sky and another arm, a boy's, came reaching across from the other side of the sky. Both arms were wrapped in barbed wire and reached for each other. That was all Francis could remember. He didn't know what it meant and hesitated to think about it too much, but it haunted him.

Francis finished his meal, laid a few wrinkled bills on the table, and hauled himself and his bag back out into the cold. A crushed velvet night covered him, and he stared into its million eyes—"God's peepholes," as his grandmother once called them. The frigid night air filled his lungs and he turned toward the *Crystal Grape*, lighting another cigarette.

The half-lit neon sign whirred and popped, making the little shambled building stand out in the shadows like a kind of beacon. A faded "Help Wanted" sign rattled against a storm window.

"Sometimes you have to do something risky to make sure you're still alive." Sarah's words rolled around in what was left of Francis' pinball mind. He stood in the quiet moonlight and looked down the desolate stretch of road that brought him to this place. Putting out his cigarette, Francis turned and walked back inside.

4   *When Jesus Came to the Cracker Barrel*

It was another bustling Cracker Barrel Tuesday morning. Four friends shuffled in from the cold toward the round table in the corner, the one where they had met for breakfast each week, going on thirty years strong. Tammy met them as she always did with hellos and hot coffee.

Although their given names were Lee, Craig , Adrian and Calvin, they often relied on the nicknames they had tagged each other with—Shades, White Shoes, Prof, and Killer—as they bantered back and forth. It was always open season for a little ribbing until Killer restored order by leading them in "The Prayer of the Holy Spirit," followed by a brief blessing for the food that would soon be set before them. Sports talk, news of the day, along with a funny recollection and a joke or two, were followed by prayer concerns as they ate.

Tammy had just refilled their coffee cups when a fellow approached the table and introduced himself. "Hi guys. Name's Jess. Mind if I join you?"

There was a moment of awkward silence as the four compadres looked the stranger over. He appeared to be in his mid-forties. He wore a sweatshirt hoodie. His work jeans were well-worn as were his hiking boots. His weathered face and dark brown eyes were framed by a salt and pepper beard and a Red Cross baseball hat that had seen better days.

"Have a seat, Jess," Shades said, followed by different versions of "sit down and join us" from the other three men.

"What would you like to eat?" Prof inquired, rising from his chair. "I'll go find Tammy."

The stranger smiled and motioned for him to sit down. "Thanks anyway, but a cup of coffee will do me just fine when Tammy comes back around."

Momentary silence returned, broken by White Shoes introducing himself. "I'm Adrian."

Pointing to the others, he continued. "He's Craig and Lee's to your right and Calvin's to your left.

"Is there anything we can do for you?"

Tammy handed Jess a steaming cup of coffee. Thanking her, he took a sip and smiled. "Just a little conversation will do for now. I saw you folks over here having a good time and thought I might sit with you for a spell."

"We're glad to have you join us," Craig chimed in, "but I'm not sure if hanging out with this bunch will do anything for your reputation."

Jess laughed. "I like hanging out with folks and meeting all kinds of people in all kinds of places, even those with suspect reputations. You might say it's kind of a hobby of mine. I couldn't help but overhear you calling Adrian 'White Shoes.' That's a nickname I've never heard before."

"It comes from when he played college football," Calvin replied.

Adrian shifted in his chair. "I was a wide receiver. Although I wasn't that fast, I had pretty good hands when it came to catching the football."

"I recall that wasn't the only thing you had pretty good hands with," Lee chimed in, to the laughter of the others.

"What about you?" Calvin asked. "Do you have any nicknames your friends ever tagged you with?"

"Quite a few, actually," Jess replied, "Some good and some not so good. I'm on the road a lot so I meet a lot of different folks," he continued, taking another sip of coffee.

"You a long-haul truck driver?" Craig inquired.

Jess held his cup out to Tammy who was making another round for more refills. "No, driving big Semis is not for me. Guess you could say if I'm anything, I'm a long-haul construction worker."

Craig took a bite of hash-brown casserole and looked up. "What kind of construction?"

"Carpentry," Jess replied.

Lee sopped up the last of the gravy with what was left of his biscuit. "That's a good skill. Our church mission trips depend on good carpenters. We found out the hard way that not everyone who thinks he is a good carpenter, is in fact, a good carpenter."

Jess laughed. "You got that right. Mission trips are a good way to help folks in need. I've always been partial to them myself. And sometimes, a good hammer is hard to find."

He pushed his chair back. "Fellows, I need to hit the John. Be back in a few minutes."

The four friends watched Jess walk toward the bathroom.

Calvin looked at his three friends. "Something's going on here. I'm not sure what it is. I'm not even sure I want to know what it is."

Craig leaned forward. "I'm feeling uneasy myself."

"Actually, fellows, I would like to get up and leave, but at the same time, for some strange reason, I feel like I have to stay—at least, until he leaves," Lee replied.

Adrian nodded in agreement. "I feel the same way the rest of you do. When he comes back, we can chat with him a few more minutes and then ease on out."

"Good idea," Lee responded. "Truth is, I do have an appointment at the Chevy dealership to get my wife's car serviced."

When Jess returned, he sat down and looked at the men. "I want you boys to know that I really appreciate your hospitality." When he told them he had picked up the check for their breakfast, they all assured him that wasn't necessary.

He looked at them and smiled. "I am happy to buy your breakfast, and I've enjoyed our time together."

"But . . .", Craig began.

Jess waved his protest off. "Don't worry about it. I am used to paying folks' bills."

Jess paused and looked intently at each man. Reaching into the pocket of his sweatshirt, he pulled out four folded pieces of paper.

"Adrian, Craig, Lee, and Calvin, I do have need of your help. I know you are good men and that you care about others. And I know what I am about to say to you is going to make you feel uneasy, even a bit strange. All I ask is that you hear me out."

Handing each of them a note, he continued. "I know each of you in a way that you may find difficult to understand. Each of these notes is personal. Each one reveals something that you have never told anyone. I want you to read them now."

The apprehension on the four friends' faces was palpable as they read what Jess had written to each of them.

Lee and Adrian's hands trembled as they laid their notes on the table. A thin bead of sweat broke out on the forehead of Craig, and Calvin rubbed his eyes as he placed the note in his shirt pocket.

"Who are you?" Calvin asked Jess.

Jess sighed and smiled. "I think you may already know, or at least suspect."

Rubbing his beard, he continued. "I am aware that what you are feeling right now is unsettling, maybe even a bit frightening. You all probably would like to get up and leave. Although you are free to do that, I hope you won't. I hope you will hear what I have to say before deciding whether to help me or not?"

"What is that you want?" Lee interjected.

Jess leaned forward. "It will require you to have faith in what you profess to believe, and in me. I need you to leave everything behind for a few weeks, your families and whatever you are doing, and meet me at a designated locale in Telford to go on a mission trip."

The four men looked at each other, no less confused than before.

Finally, Calvin spoke. "How long will this mission trip last, and why us?"

"It will last as long as it needs to last. I have chosen you for good reasons, reasons you do not understand, reasons that will require you to choose to go with me or remain behind."

"What you are telling us reminds me a lot of the parable of 'the rich young ruler,'" Calvin continued.

Jess leaned back in his chair. "You four are rich indeed, in ways you aren't even aware of, including what you can become. But no, Calvin, I'm not asking any of you to do what the rich young ruler was instructed to do."

"What would be required?" Lee replied.

Jess touched Lee's arm. "I'm not asking you to give up your money, possessions, or families. I am asking the four of you to give up your time for a few weeks and follow me on a mission trip that will help countless people, as well as provide you with a blessing unlike any joy you have ever experienced."

Several more moments of silence passed before Jess spoke.

"I won't ask for your decision right now. You can think and pray about it, and talk it over with each other. The note I gave each of you has the date, time, and directions to a barn in Telford. It will be the one with the neon cross over the entrance. I will have chairs arranged with your names on them." As the men rose from the table, Adrian asked Jess how many were needed for the mission trip.

Jess zipped up his sweatshirt. "A total of twelve. Two from your group and ten others."

Looking at the four friends, he smiled and tipped his hat. "God bless."

Then he walked away.

24

5 *Truth Teller*

Two years ago, I saw the truth.

Two years and fifteen minutes ago I started speaking it.

My life hasn't been worth a damn since.

I always heard that the truth will make you free.

Free from what? I'll tell you what. In the span of two short years, I was freed from my career, my wife, and daughter, and even from the lousy efficiency apartment I have been living in for the last two months. Hell, yes, I'm free.

Free to take my last three hundred bucks and hit the open road in a worn-out Ford Taurus, 160,000 miles young. Free from everything that made my life what it was—everything that I wanted and worked for.

Two short years ago on a cold Friday evening I was nursing my third Sam Adams and bullshitting with the regular-end-of-the-week-upper-management-wannabees for the *City Daily News*.

I was at the top of the mid-level-career food chain where I toiled for my living. A Master of Arts degree in journalism and ten years of busting my ass had brought me to the edge of greatness and to Buddy's Bar on what turned out to be a cold day in hell.

As a hard-working assistant editor in charge of the sports and features sections, I was just a skip and jump and some well-placed ass kissing away from one of the two prized associate executive editors' slots. Given the inevitability of Ed McMann's impending retirement, that soon-to-be-vacant office with its own bathroom and big picture window had my name written all over it. I had another advantage over the beer and bourbon swizzling reprobates I drank with during our Friday evening rituals. They had their eye on the same elusive prize that I did, but unlike them, I could actually write. Yeah, I was kicking ass and kissing ass—a lethal combination that pointed like a champion bird dog sitting on a covey of quail to the golden ring I was about to grab. A ring that would make me and mine proud and the envy of all the other yahoos at the *City Daily News*.

Trouble is, I drank one beer too many because it was during that third beer that fate stepped in and punctured my balloon of ambition, laying waste to life as I knew it.

During that third beer I overheard Geraldine Stevens talking to the bartender about her sorry-ass husband. Several black eyes, a neck brace, and her son's increased bed wetting had lit a fire under her that only fear and loneliness kept in check. Enough was enough. Geraldine was ready to leave the worthless son-of-a-bitch she was married to and return to her parents in South Alabama. Trouble was she was broke. As soon as she could put her hands on enough cash for two bus tickets, she and her son were heading south to freedom. At least that's what she told the bored bartender who was practicing the time-worn bartender's art of pretending to give a damn.

That's what she was telling him. But I knew better. The king-size gimlet she was sucking on was doing the talking for her and her boy. My guess was that she was at least a broken arm or preteen suicide attempt away from speaking for herself and acting like the mother she was pretending to be.

Yeah, I could see right through her. It was like I had known her all my life. And I didn't like what I saw. So be it. A quick trip to the men's room to relieve myself and I would be on my way home to Natalie and Natasha, my wife and daughter, respectively.

I even remember the sound of zipping up my Dockers and feeling the cold blast of air that hit me in the face as I stepped out to hail a cab on that armpit of a February night. As I waved my arms to no avail, none other than Geraldine, the gimlet swizzler, exited the bar and sidled up next to me. She stood too close for comfort and I didn't like the way she looked at me. It was like she wanted something. I stamped my feet against the cold and she just stood there looking at me as if she wanted to speak but was waiting for permission. I was thinking that sometimes strangers are best left strangers when she spoke.

Unlike the I'll-tell-you-a-thing-or-two voice from inside the bar, she asked me in a child's uncertain whisper, "Will you help me get a cab?"

That's what she said, but what I heard through some strange cosmic filter of fate was, "Will you HELP ME?"

Not taking my eyes off her, I stepped back in shock and *spoke.* I never do that—speak what I see.

The truth, as I see it, should stay where it belongs—in one's head. But not this time. This time it spoke me.

Offering her the contents of my wallet I said, "Geraldine, you need to leave that worthless bastard and go home to your parents before you lose yourself or worse—your son's life."

Geraldine's jaw dropped and she looked as if she were about to reply. Instead, she snatched the money out of my hand and hopped into the cab that had just pulled up as if on cue in some third-rate movie.

That's right. She took the money and got into the cab without so much as a thank you. Did she go home, retrieve her son, and take the next bus to Alabama?

Damned if I know. All I recall is that for the first time I could remember, I spoke what I saw. Holding my empty wallet, I walked home in the cold to the waiting warmth of Natalie's inquisition.

Although I stayed away from Buddy's Bar, it didn't seem to help calm my new-found affliction. The truth had me by the balls and every time it squeezed, I spoke. I wanted to keep my thoughts to myself but possessed by a clarity of insight I never imagined and an inability to remain silent, I could feel myself sinking ever deeper into the quicksand of opportunity.

Two months after my encounter with Geraldine, I elicited the same dumbfounded look of incredulity from my boss, Ned Jasper who—rumor had it—was about to appoint me associate editor. The words rushed out, dragging my reluctant voice with them.

"Ned, we've been friends a long time, but I've got to tell you, screwing that journalism intern isn't worth your twenty-year marriage to Marge, not to mention the respect of your children."

Ned's response was to the point.

"Get out!"

As it turned out, his retort foretold a wider arc of response than I ever would have anticipated. "Get out" not only referred to the immediacy of that embarrassing moment in his office, but also came to include the newspaper itself. Needless to say, I didn't get the promotion and soon after found myself reassigned to the "eastern front" of newspaper work reporting on city commission and board meetings.

The day I finally resigned, I tried to explain to Natalie that personal integrity was more important than a promotion or a particular kind of job. Her expression of disapproval fed the hidden part of me that agreed with her. Six months and a series of unsuccessful interviews and substitute teaching assignments later, Natalie uttered what has become a refrain in my life. Between sips of orange juice, Natalie's mouth opened and Ned Jasper's voice seemed to speak through her early morning smoker's rasp. "Get out!" So I did.

I left it all behind, not willingly, but of necessity. Even Natasha shed no tears the day I left with suitcase in hand. The last sound I heard was a good riddance bark from Bobo, the cocker spaniel.

In short order, I went from writing for the newspaper to delivering newspapers. My pre-dawn route combined with education's constant need for inner city substitute teachers, afforded me the luxury of a well-worn efficiency on 10th Avenue and evening forays to Buddy's, where Mike, the bartender, offered me the same courtesy he had given to Geraldine a year earlier.

My friend, Sam Adams, was too rich for my current financial fortunes so I mingled with his more budget-minded kin and attempted to sort out what had become of my life. I confided to Mike that at least I was reasonably confident that things couldn't get any worse.

I was wrong.

I struck up an ill-fated friendship with my landlord, Buck LePew. Buck apparently saw some semblance of the management potential in me that Ned and my former wife had given up on. In exchange for managing the eight-unit apartment house I resided in, I got to live rent-free.

A spark of my former self slowly began to re-emerge as I considered my future prospects in the field of residential management. As I became more familiar with Buck's enterprise, I soon realized that some rocks were best not overturned. A clear pattern emerged of compounding the misery of elderly tenants on fixed incomes by excessively raising their rent and ignoring their pleas for repairs and basic service. Forcing such undesirables out of their apartments allowed the vacated units to be rented to higher paying young professionals.

Even as I tried to maintain control, I could feel that ugly entity known as a conscience beginning to awaken and take shape. It wouldn't be long before my tongue would begin to work its black magic.

I still remember the day Buck LePew, chewing nervously on a cigar stub, was held captive by the logic of truth's outpouring.

I had just finished an impressive oration that concluded by my telling Buck that he was too good of a person to torture his elderly residents for nothing more than a little extra filthy lucre, not to mention that what he did to them, good or bad, would be returned to him ten-fold.

Buck LePew said two things in response to my well-intentioned query. His first response was, "Who the hell do you think you are, some crazy-ass prophet?" Then he uttered those dreaded, oft-spoken words.

"Get Out!"

I still remember the last moments I spent at Buck's establishment. My bag was packed and positioned next to the door, and I stood in the bathroom, looking out the window. I was lost in my thoughts. Not just in my thoughts, it was me that was lost. I had nowhere to go. I had nothing. I was nothing.

I peered out of the frost-encrusted window and all I could see was a barren bush with a single branch reaching toward me. On the end of it was a single bud.

My wet face pressed against the glass.

It was a beautiful thing.

6 Sunday Biscuits

Mildred Percy stood at her kitchen window— the one decorated with ceramic thimbles donated by her third-grade Sunday school class—and watched the parking lot lights across the street snuff out one by one. It was getting late.

She walked to the kitchen screen door, one hand caked in Bisquick and the other holding a bottle of sorghum molasses. Her husband, Elmer, liked biscuits for supper on Sunday evenings. He would often joke to his six p.m. Sunday night congregation that the evening's sermon may be cut short because it was biscuit night.

Tonight, though, it was getting late; the clock was creeping past eight-thirty.

"Elmer! It's close to suppertime," Mildred shouted in a voice so loud it surprised her.

Five minutes ticked by and still no sign of her husband. She looked out at the old oak tree in the back yard, its branches lifted by a late summer breeze, as if it were shrugging its shoulders, saying, "I don't know where he is either." Mildred smiled at that thought for a quick moment and returned her attention to her missing husband. She knew he'd grunt and groan if the biscuits and sorghum weren't on the table by the time her grandmother's clock struck five o'clock. She didn't mind it so much–the biscuits, that is, not the clock. She had always hated the sound that clock made.

Slamming the screen door behind her, Mildred hurried to the garden where she found Elmer, crumpled on the ground, his legs spread and his back against the old oak. He was holding the gold office pen he always had clipped to his shirt pocket, the one she got him for Christmas, with his name engraved on it. His thumb was nervously clicking the pen.

"Mr. Percy, what in the world is going on with you. Those biscuits are gonna crawl back in the bowl if you don't come eat 'em!" Mildred arched her eyebrow in disapproval and placed her Bisquick-caked hand on her hip, just like her mother used to do. She hated when her mother did that.

"Something happened to me Milly," Elmer said in a soft voice, wiping at eyes, wet and raw with tears.

Mildred's wrinkled brow softened and she could feel her heartbeat begin to race. A warm breeze lifted the hair off her neck and carried with it the unmistakable scent of burning biscuits. She mourned them for a split second.

"Well Lord have mercy, do I need to call Dr. Elsey, or 911?" she asked her husband.

Elmer shook his head and ran his hand through the tall grass beside him. He bit his lower lip-a lifelong nervous habit of his, the words in his throat falling apart before making their way to his mouth. He breathed deeply and watched clouds move across the sky. He thought for a moment about how he had never noticed the sky before.

Mildred hesitantly took his hand. He could feel her worry moving over him.

"What's going on with you, Elmer Percy?" she asked with soft urgency. "You want to come inside and talk about it? Those biscuits are..."

Elmer gave her hand a slight squeeze and looked up at her.

"I think I had a dream."

"A dream? What kind of a dream?"

Elmer sighed and ran his hand through the grass again. He shook his head slowly, watching the sun drop a couple of rungs down the sky.

"Don't know," he answered. "I took a rest here at the oak for a spell after checking on the garden. Must've dozed off. Can't say for sure what happened after that."

He picked a hand full of grass and let it get swept up by a wisp of evening breeze.

Mildred breathed deep and picked at the dried biscuit mix on her hand. Some of it had gotten in her watch and she drew her lips tight in mild frustration. She liked that watch.

"You want to tell me what you dreamed?" she asked, rubbing her forehead with her clean hand. A few moments passed without an answer, and Mildred sat down in a thatch of tall grass beside her husband. She could feel his hand shaking.

"I guess so," he finally responded. "I'm not sure you'll understand, and . . . well, it's pretty crazy. I'm not sure I understand it myself. Must have been asleep, but–can't explain it–I felt . . . awake. More awake than usual. In the dream I was standing in this crowd of people – all kind of people, young, old, and folks our age. And they were laughing and carryin' on–and dancing. They were dancing to that rock and roll fuss that I used to say was the devil's dance and the reason deaf people never had it so good."

Mildred let slip a slight smile.

"Well, you can bet your biscuits I wanted to leave that place as fast as I could," Elmer continued. "But even though I wanted to leave, my feet wouldn't move."

He reached down and touched his ankle. Mildred's eyes followed his hand.

"The people looked so happy and then I noticed they were all looking at one person who was dancing and laughing with them. Then the person they were looking at looked at me, and . . ."

Mildred reached to touch her husband's temple, turned gray by two heart attacks, a wayward daughter and a few bad breaks that could have gone either way.

"Milly, this sounds awful crazy," Elmer said, shaking his head. "I just . . ."

Elmer paused, his voice, the once-commanding baritone one would expect from a veteran preacher such as himself, disappearing into a hoarse, almost childlike whisper. It was a rare moment of vulnerability, and for Mildred, it did not go unnoticed.

She sat still in the tall grass that swayed side to side in the dying dusk light, holding her husband's trembling hand. Her eyes traced the old wrinkled lines and she thought about when those hands held their child for the first time, and how they helped bury her mother when she passed away from liver cancer, and how they could also be swift and fierce.

"Tell me what happened," she said, watching tears streak her husband's cheeks.

Elmer breathed deep and turned his head away from his wife, wiping his face. "Well, the person looking back at me was Him."

"Him who?"

Elmer's voice softened.

"Jesus."

Mildred stroked his thumb with her forefinger.

"At first I couldn't believe it," Elmer said, "but he was looking at me, drawing me into the laughter, even though I fought against it, at first. Then he walked over to me and spoke only once."

"What did he say?" Mildred asked, her hand now resting still on top of her husband's.

"He said, 'Where's Mildred?'"

Mildred withdrew her hand from his and slipped it into her pocket.

"Before I could say anything, he took my hand and we began to dance. I couldn't believe it. I felt like a little boy, like when I used to dance with my mother in her kitchen. It's like he reached in, dusted off that memory, and made it new again. There I was dancing with Jesus, and I found myself laughing and singing with him and the others."

Elmer paused a moment, biting down softly on his lower lip. "Then Jesus stopped dancing even though the others continued. Then he looked at me in a different way."

Elmer's words trailed off, and a sudden, unfamiliar sadness overcame him.

Mildred patted his hand.

"His eyes changed. I became afraid. I didn't want to look but knew I had to. Can't explain why. I just knew."

"What did they look like—his eyes," Mildred asked.

Elmer's face crinkled into a thinking mode, his thoughts on a quest to honor his wife's question.

"They were burning," he said, "like the last embers of a fire, glowing around the edges but dark in the center—death's eyes. Even though I looked away, his eyes looked into me, through me probin' around into places I had forgotten. Places safe from eyes. But there he was, lookin'—his eyes were like searchlights, seeing everything. I couldn't hide. I tell you, I've never been so ashamed and scared in my life. No matter how tight I held on, those eyes pulled every piece of darkness out of me and set it right down on the front row, then switched on the spotlight. Like the time my father beat me when I was twelve with a leather harness 'cause I had lied to him. He said he was beating the devil out of me, but it hurt so bad that ever since, I felt that anything good had to hurt, that sometimes you had to deny and even hurt the body to save the soul. Like the time I whipped Julie when she was fifteen after I caught her drinking beer with her friends."

Elmer breathed deeply and wiped his brow with his shirt sleeve. Leaning his head back against the old oak tree, he continued. "And there was the time after we were engaged, I sneaked over to Embreeville to see an old girlfriend."

Elmer paused, anticipating a reaction, but was met with only silence.

"I never told you about that and I'm sorry. I'm not that kind of man, and I know you know that. But in that dream, I felt like death had a hold of my belt-loops."

As his words burrowed through her ears, Mildred looked at the fading sun in the distance; her grief hung still in the air like stale laundry on a line.

They both fell silent for a while. An evening breeze picked up and rustled the leaves above them. The sun traded places with the moon.

Mildred put her hands in her pockets and stood up. The tall grass fell against her ankles.

"Mildred, I looked into his eyes and my heart broke in two."

Tears rolled down Elmer's cheeks as his voice cracked and dropped to a whisper. "Then his eyes changed again. I was bathed in the look of those eyes . . . like a newborn baby." The moon blinked in between clouds passing across the sky and Mildred closed her eyes in its light. "Ovenlight," she thought.

She looked at her hands. They were swollen and sore.

Mildred started off through the tall grass back toward the kitchen door. Elmer turned to look in her direction. He counted silently each step she made.

She stopped and turned to look back at him.

"I'll put some more biscuits in the oven," she said. "Come help me set the table."

7   *Special of the Week*

"It's cold as a witch's teat out there," Jimmy "Fastball" Burns exclaimed as he bustled through the main entrance of "Everybody Rides" used car lot, passing out cheeseburgers, fries and steaming cups of coffee.

"I ain't never seen a cold spell like this in the middle of December."

"You got that right!" Sam Jenkins, who was also known as Sam "Batboy" Jenkins, chimed in.

Buzz "Homerun" Renfro took a sip of coffee. "Why don't you two yahoos shut up and pass me some fries before they get cold."

J.J. "Coach" Moran, the Manager, looked at the three salesmen with mild disgust, the way a father would look at his rambunctious children. "Why don't all three of you quiet down so I can finish this here book on Joe DiMaggio, the greatest baseball player who ever lived."

"Everybody Rides" was actually the budget used car lot of the mega-dealership, "King of the Road Jaguar/Chrysler/Dodge/Kia/Daewoo." In automobile sales, this was the bottom of the barrel. The good used cars were on display in a paved lot adjoining the new car dealership. "Everybody Rides" was located two blocks from the other lots. "King of the Road" owner, Wild Bill Hancock, didn't want a car lot that proudly displayed in bright red letters under its name—

NOTHING OVER $3995 and YOUR JOB IS YOUR CREDIT— to be too closely associated with the classier side of his business. As added punishment, "Everybody Rides" had to stay open until 10:00 p.m. each night while the rest of the dealership closed at 9:00 p.m.

If an outside observer concluded that Coach had a thing for baseball, he or she would be right on the money. He had coached Little League baseball for over thirty years and never had a winning season, but to hear him tell it, he had always been one hit or pitch away from baseball glory.

The only sounds in the office that evening were the sounds of four men inhaling their supper as they chewed, gulped, and belched their way down to the last French fry. Each man had his own story of what brought him to this place. Coach had successfully managed the upscale used car lot for ten years before he punched out an opposing Little League coach who happened to be the cousin of Wild Bill Hancock. The others were exiled to "Everybody Rides" for different reasons and in keeping with his passion for baseball, Coach had given each of his "players" a nickname.

Jimmy "Fastball" Burns had been the leading Dodge truck salesman for three years in a row. Nobody knew more about pickup trucks than he did and nobody could close a truck sale as quickly as he could. Unfortunately, "Fastball" decided to celebrate his third divorce by driving off in a brand-new loaded Dodge Club Cab that he hadn't cleared with the manager. With a fifth of Jim Beam riding shotgun, he totaled the truck and his sales career.

Sam "Batboy" Jenkins was a wiry fellow with nervous eyes. Coach had named him "Batboy" because as he frequently reminded him: "Boy, you ain't even in the game. You can't score, if you don't get to the plate." Coach used to call him "Third String" Jenkins, but after three consecutive months at the bottom of the sales ladder, demoted him to "Batboy."

Sam was the only one of the four men who had never been married. In fact, he had allegedly had only two dates and one didn't count—the occasion of his senior prom when he paid his next-door neighbor, Debbie Ann Humburger, twenty dollars to accompany him. Rumor had it that he offered to pay her another five dollars for a goodnight kiss. The truth was that Debbie Ann told Sam that the only part of her he could kiss for five dollars was her ass.

Coach was married to his second wife; "Fast ball" was, as he liked to put it, currently "playing the field"; and Buzz, also divorced, was heavily involved with Darlene, a former dancer with "Sand and Sun Cruise Lines." She was presently employed as senior nail technician for "The New You Salon."

Buzz and Darlene had been going together for more than a year, and although he had told no one, he was planning to pop the question on New Year's Eve.

Leaning back in an office chair with his feet propped up on his desk, Buzz fingered the gold-plated money clip in his left front pocket that secured the five, one-hundred-dollar bills he had saved to buy Darlene's engagement ring. He smiled in anticipation of her excitement. No one could get as excited as Darlene. Buzz's daydream was abruptly interrupted by the grating voice of Jimmy "Fastball" Burns.

"Customer on the lot. It's your turn Renfro," he bellowed. Buzz lit a Marlboro Light and peered out the office window into the cold, black December night. Who would be looking for a used car at 8:45 p.m. on a cold Saturday night? Blowing a spiral of smoke rings toward the ceiling, Buzz said, "Why don't we give them a few minutes to see if they are really serious."

Without taking his eyes off the page he was reading, Coach took charge of the situation: "Batter up Renfro. Get your ass out there and into scoring position. Batboy, you're in the on-deck circle."

Batboy grinned at Buzz. "I done taken a peek Homerun. I can tell from here, she ain't much to look at and more'n likely she ain't got no money. Them two kids means she ain't got no man which means she ain't got no money which means you ain't gonna make no money. *Comprendez, Amigo?*"

Buzz blew another series of smoke rings toward the door. "Two things, Batboy: First, I'm not your *Amigo* and second, can you *comprendez* that?"

Zipping up his parka, Buzz ground out the remnants of his cigarette in the ashtray, closed the door behind him, and stepped out into the cold night.

Agnes was cold and not just from the threadbare parka she was wearing, but cold deep inside, down in her bones. She felt like her heart was almost frozen shut—like it was barely beating. The only thing on this freezing December night that gave her any warmth was her son, Kenny, and her daughter, Sonja. And they gave her just enough to keep her going a while longer. Ten years seemed like a lifetime ago when she up and married their father, a truck driver twenty years her senior. They met at the small mountain top café where she had worked as a waitress. Harold had promised her the good life, but what he had given her was too many years of misery. He finally left her and the children two years ago with unpaid bills and no goodbyes.

Agnes wasn't a woman given to bitterness, she was just tired. Somehow, having Kenny and Sonja made the misery worth the trouble. Ages eight and six, they were still young enough to make up the difference between the poverty and hopelessness with a few well-practiced dreams, the most recent incarnation being what Santa Claus might bring them. At least it seemed to be so as far as Sonja was concerned. Agnes wasn't as sure about Kenny. He acted happy enough, but she had seen the sad, uncertain look in his eyes when he thought she wasn't paying attention.

Working two jobs, one at a nursing home and the other at Taco Bell didn't make for much of a life. They had been evicted from their apartment for unpaid rent three days after her truck had been repossessed. Agnes had no illusions about her chances of getting the salesman walking towards her to sell her a car for a fifty-dollar down payment, but fifty dollars was all she had.

"How do you do, Ma'am? You gotta a couple of fine-looking children. Name's Buzz Renfro. What can I do for you?"

Agnes looked at the salesman for several moments before she spoke. "Mr. Renfro, my name's Agnes Davis and these here are my children, Kenny and Sonja. We are in great need of a reliable vehicle."

"Yes ma'am. Well, you've come to the right place because 'reliable' is our middle name. Every vehicle we sell has undergone a 21-point inspection."

"Mama," Sonja interrupted, "I'm hungry!"

"Hush Sonja, we'll get something to eat when we finish our business with Mr. Renfro."

Dropping her head at the tone of reprimand in Agnes's voice, Sonja buried her face in Kenny's jacket.

"Tell you what kids, how 'bout candy bars and cokes on me while your mother and I check out the cars," Buzz offered, pulling three one dollar bills out of his pocket.

"I couldn't let you do that, Mr. Renfro," Agnes protested.

"I ain't hungry anyway," Kenny added, stuffing his hands in the pockets of his denim jacket.

"Well, I am," Sonja exclaimed, peering from behind the folds of her brother's jacket.

"Hey, I insist," Buzz responded. "Besides, you'll be warm inside. Ask for a Mr. Moran when you get inside. He'll show you where the goodies are."

Agnes relented, and Kenny took the three dollars and Sonja by the hand and proceeded toward the office. Buzz lit another cigarette as he and Agnes stood watching the vapor trail of Kenny and Sonja's breathing as they made their way toward food and warmth. "Now, Mrs. Davis, what would you like to look at? We only have about an hour until we close."

Agnes' eyes escorted her children into the office. "Mr. Renfro, I'm going to be honest with you. I'm in desperate need of a vehicle. I have two children, two jobs—if I can come up with transportation—nowhere to live, and fifty dollars in my right coat pocket."

Buzz took a deep draw from his cigarette before he spoke.

"Ma'am, please don't take this the wrong way, but sounds to me like you need a lot more help than just a vehicle—at least more help than I can give you. You need to get a hold of some area churches or the Human Services Department or something else like that. Besides, the cheapest vehicle on our lot requires a down payment of several hundred dollars. Maybe you ought to call your family."

Agnes turned her head slightly to compose herself. "No offense taken, Mr. Renfro. Don't have no family, but I'll figure something out."

She took a deep breath and extended her hand. "I want to thank you for the kindness you showed my children. I'll be fetchin' them now."

"Well, Ma'am, at least let me get you a hot cup of coffee."

"Thank you, but that won't be necessary," Agnes replied as she walked toward the office, leaving Buzz to ponder the crisp night air.

"Hellfire," Buzz muttered to himself. "Why do I always have to get the hard-luck customers? Life's tough for everybody."

He could see Kenny's and Sonja's faces peering out of the office window as their mother approached them and thought to himself, where will they go? What'll happen to them? What does it matter to me? It doesn't.

All Buzz had on his mind was the wad of cash in his pocket and Darlene. He popped a piece of chewing gum in his mouth and pretended to check the cars on the lot. He also pretended it would be less embarrassing for Agnes and her kids if he waited until they left.

Buzz watched as Agnes and her children made their way across the car lot toward the bus stop on the corner. As they started to cross the street, Sonja turned and waved to him and shouted, "Hey Mister! Thank you for the candy. I hope you have a Merry Christmas!"

It was at that precise moment that Buzz Renfro went temporarily insane.

He might as well have been hit by a meteor from outer space. The gold-plated money clip in his pants pocket seemed to turn white hot. He felt dizzy, his knees buckled slightly, and even with the chill of the night air, Buzz could feel a bead of sweat break out on his forehead.

Somewhere between Sonja's "Merry" and "Christmas," something—some great mystery—traveling faster than the speed of light, had penetrated Buzz Renfro and knocked him senseless. In that moment, the fake gold nugget ring on his right hand ceased to exist. Even the image of Darlene became little more than a dancing shadow. Buzz was pulled out of himself into a place he had never been before. It was as if he was having an out-of-body experience, observing himself running toward Agnes and her two children who were standing under the street light, waiting on the rest of their lives.

As he ran, his mind was saying *stop*, but his legs weren't listening.

When he caught up with them, Buzz bent over and grabbed his knees, breathing heavily.

"Mr. Renfro, are you all-right?"

Buzz took a deep breath, sucking cold air into his lungs. "Yes ma'am, I believe I am. It just occurred to me that we might have a vehicle suitable to your needs."

"But I told you, I only have . . ."

Buzz interrupted her, "I forgot to tell you about our special of the week. If you could use a 1992 minivan, you could drive it away tonight for no down payment and one hundred and twenty-five dollars a month."

"I don't know what to say," Agnes' eyes widened.

"Say yes, Mama. Say yes!" Sonja exclaimed, jumping up and down as Kenny looked on silently.

"Yes," Agnes said, her face freed up the hint of a smile, the first she had felt in weeks.

43

Agnes with her coffee and Kenny and Sonja with their hot chocolate waited in the customer lounge while Buzz filled out the paperwork.

Batboy shook his head. "I would've bet a month's pay that lady wouldn't have two cents to her name. Can't believe she's got the cash for the down payment."

"Well believe it," Buzz replied as he signed the last of the finance forms.

Draining the last of his coffee, Coach looked solemnly at Buzz and cleared his throat, "Well, Homerun, it wasn't one of our better units—certainly not of home-run caliber, but I will give you an infield hit."

Buzz handed Agnes the keys. Even Kenny seemed excited. Not like Sonja, but at least pleased. Looking at the keys in her hand, Agnes didn't say anything. Instead, she put her arms around Buzz and placed her head on his chest. He didn't know what else to do, so he hugged her.

As the minivan left the lot of "Everybody Rides," all Buzz could see was the smiling face of Sonja pressed against the rear window. Her smile went right through him. His fingers grazed the empty money clip. It wasn't hot anymore. And he knew Darlene probably wouldn't be coming down his chimney on Christmas Eve.

Opening a fresh pack of cigarettes, Buzz looked up at the glittering stars and said to no one in particular, "Merry 'Hotdamn' Christmas."

8 *Invisible Boy*

Although wavy blond hair and clear blue eyes gave Teddy a strange sort of handsome, "five foot two, eyes of blue" was not a description that lived up to a teenage boy's testosterone dreams. To make matters worse, Teddy was not a particularly good name for a fifteen-year-old boy of slight build trying to prove his mettle in a one-street, blue-collar subdivision. And if his name and physique weren't enough of a handicap, his family's well-worn, single-wide trailer stood out like a sore thumb in the sea of split-foyer, ranch, and two-story stick-built houses.

The adults in the neighborhood weren't about to roll out the red carpet for the trailer family perched on a kind of no-man's land in a cornfield just on edge of the subdivision's boundary, but they had just enough decency to accommodate to some extent, the family's lonely son.

Teddy's story was originally told to Little Jack, the neighborhood renegade and closest thing to a friend Teddy would ever have. His story filtered its way from Little Jack's parents to the Smiths, then the Johnsons, and on to the Bartholomew's until everyone in the neighborhood had heard it at least twice, everyone except old man Murphy who had stayed to himself in a vinyl-clad, split-foyer ever since his wife Norma died.

Of course, as Teddy's story made its way through the various families, it took a number of twists and turns, exaggerations both added and subtracted. The gist of it is as follows: When Teddy was eight years old, his Daddy drank whiskey and beat and abused his mother while he and his younger sister were forced to watch.

When in a drunken state, his father was fond of threatening to do in his mother, sister, and himself with his good friends Smith and Wesson. Weary of his relentless abuse, Teddy's mother decided to turn his father's friends against him.

Three times these friends spoke his name and three times he watched the red, concentric holes appear on his mid-section. He only uttered one word during the entire ordeal and he only said it once. After the first shot rang out, he shouted, "Teddy!"

Teddy and his sister looked on in silence as their father fell against the living room wall and slid down it, clutching what was left of his Bud-Lite and watching its contents mingle with the blood pouring from his belly onto the lime-green shag carpet.

Two years later, Teddy's mother married his current stepfather, and two years after that they moved onto no-man's land.

Although Teddy and his mother had never spoken of the killing, and as much as he believed in his own mind that his father deserved what he got, one thing had always bothered him about the incident. He didn't like the way his dying father spoke to him. He didn't like being called by name as if he were some kind of official witness—as if he could have done something about the shooting. If Teddy hadn't been called out by his dying daddy, he could have remained invisible. Of course, to the parents in the neighborhood, he was still for the most part invisible, but not so much that they wouldn't invite him in when he knocked on their front doors looking for refuge and a prospective playmate.

Still, the welcome mats, one after another, were eventually withdrawn because Teddy—like anyone dyingof an unquenchable thirst—couldn't stop drinking from any sign of friendship and kindness that was offered, no matter how small or fragile. So on he went, from one house and playmate to another. As he searched for the next sign of hospitality, what he left behind looked like a clear-cut forest. Whatever his circumstance, no matter how many doors were closed to him and how few were open, there was always one place Teddy was accepted or at least tolerated—the basketball court at the end of the street.

In the cul-de-sac on Muskgrove Lane, a portable basketball goal and backboard stood guard like a silent sentinel and waited. Around 3:30 each afternoon, Monday through Friday, you could hear it coming before you saw it. An ancient yellow school bus slowly belched its way down the single curved road of Muskgrove Lane and expelled its prisoners, free until 6:45 the following morning.

They came out of that bus like rats leaving a sinking ship—first grade through high school. The youth of the neighborhood sauntered and ran toward the houses that beckoned them with the promise of snacks and juice. Thirty minutes later, the rhythmic thumping of basketballs sounded like a war chant and signaled that the games were about to begin.

Younger boys watched older ones dribble basketballs between their legs, make fancy lay-up shots, and attempt the occasional, but rarely successful, dunk. Boys and the several girls who braved the hallowed court raised their hands and voices, begging to be picked. But their cries to be chosen fell on deaf ears. To the older boys of Muskgrove Lane, they had been designated the Peanut Gallery, spectators one and all—spectators not players. Nothing more needed to be said. The best the members of the Peanut Gallery could hope for Monday through Friday was the brief window of opportunity that presented itself between games. Their reward for being loyal and appreciative spectators was the possibility of five minutes of wild abandon on the court while the real players took a water break at the end of each game. The brief melee only faintly resembled the game of basketball.

Although Teddy was old enough to qualify as a real player, he wasn't chosen—partly because of his questionable athletic skills, but most importantly because of his penchant for combing his hair when he was supposed to be guarding a player from the opposing team. Every few minutes, Teddy would reach for the comb protruding from his back pocket. It was like a personal appearance compulsion. Teddy would raise his left hand in defense while he carefully combed his blond tresses with his right hand.

It is no secret that one-armed basketball defenders don't fare well when their opponent dribbles past them while they are in mid-stroke for an easy layup. And no amount of laughter and derision from the older boys seemed to deter Teddy from his compulsion. So, he was exiled Monday through Friday to the Peanut Gallery where he could comb in peace.

There was also one other more subtle, unspoken reason why Teddy wasn't picked to play in the real games.

Technically, he wasn't a member of Muskgrove Lane and since it was important to many of the adults in Muskgrove Lane that Teddy and his family knew their place, it was also important to their children. The one exception was Little Jack. As the neighborhood rebel, he stood on more than one occasion as Teddy's sole defender. Although he was shorter than Teddy, he was a fierce competitor on the court and was known for starting fights that he knew he couldn't win.

Most of the boys in Muskgrove Lane, younger and older, were not inclined to rile up Little Jack because of his volatile nature, but even Little Jack couldn't get Teddy out of the Peanut Gallery. His one vote simply wasn't enough, and besides, he didn't really want Teddy playing on his team. On Monday through Friday Teddy couldn't play, he could only watch, but on Saturday, things were different.

On Saturday, Detective Burns played. He was the only father in the neighborhood that was a Saturday regular. While the other fathers cut their grass, fished and golfed, Lloyd Burns played basketball with a bunch of kids. In fact, his wife, Myrtle, on more than one occasion indicated to the Detective that he was nothing more than a big kid himself. Of course, her comments went in one ear and out the other. While Lloyd loved his wife dearly, as far as sports were concerned, Myrtle definitely belonged in the Peanut Gallery.

All the kids and teenagers of Muskgrove Lane referred to Detective Lloyd Burns as "Sarge" in deference to his slight limp, the result of a wound he received in Vietnam and for which he received a Purple Heart. In truth, Sarge was admired not so much because he had received a combat medal or was a Police

Detective, but because he could dunk the basketball with either hand whenever he felt like it. He designated his trademark dunk as the "Muskgrove Megadunk" or "M and M" for short.

Although he was judicious in its use, he always demonstrated the "M and M" once or twice each Saturday to the squeals and delight of the "Peanut Gallery." On Saturdays, Sarge was also the Team Captain and Referee. More importantly, he always made sure everyone got to play. His authority and skill were unquestioned.

Sometimes Sarge's team would win and sometimes it wouldn't, but to the bewilderment of the older, more talented players, Sarge always chose the same person first to be on his team. He always chose Teddy. The Monday-through-Friday spectator was always the first one chosen on Saturday by the neighborhood Superstar.

Sarge's only requirement was that Teddy hand over his comb for the duration of the morning's game. The older boys looked at each other and shook their heads in disgust as Teddy proudly took his place beside Sarge at Center Court. No one ever knew why Sarge always chose Teddy first. Teddy imagined that Sarge saw some hidden talent in him that wasn't apparent to the others, but then Teddy had always had a vivid and overactive imagination.

Sarge was every bit the Field General on Saturday mornings, preferring to pass the ball and set picks for his younger teammates from the Peanut Gallery. And the Monday-through-Friday All-Stars knew if they got too rambunctious or aggressive with Sarge's teammates, they would end up eating one of his "M and M's." Sarge would bark orders to his charges as if they were on a do-or-die combat mission.

"Teddy, guard your flank! PJ's moving to your right!"
"Hands up, Joey!"
"Defense team, Defense!"
"Shoot, Susie, Shoot!"

On Saturdays, the bonds of oppression were cut loose, and the spirits of the weekday underclass soared. They imagined they were also players. When the lucky shot was rewarded with the swoosh of the net, they could count on a smile and a wink from Sarge.

"Money in the bank," Sarge would reply, giving the one who scored a "high-five."

On Saturdays, Teddy most of all, came alive for a few hours. On that day, he stood in the light and heard the applause and was called by his name. Unfortunately, Saturday only came once a week. There were six other days in between.

Then one Saturday, Teddy began to change.

Everyone had headed toward home except Sarge, Teddy and Little Jack. Sarge decided that the two of them needed some extra help with their free-throw shooting.

"Hey Sarge, Teddy says he's gonna become a Ninja," Little Jack commented as he threw up another errant free-throw. "That so?" asked Sarge.

Sarge gathered up the rebound and passed the ball to Teddy.

"Yeah," chortled Little Jack. "Teddy's done ordered his uniform."

Teddy bounced the basketball two times, then swished it through the net.

"That so, Teddy?" Sarge queried, throwing the basketball to Little Jack.

Teddy pulled his comb out of his back pocket and began to run it through his hair.

"Yes Sir, Sarge. I'm gonna earn my black belt in Ninja."

Sarge leaned back against the pole that held up the backboard. "Teddy, how you gonna do that, become a Ninja?"

Teddy's eyes lit up in a way Sarge had never seen before. His enthusiasm drew in Little Jack as well. It was like Teddy had found something important that he had been looking for and had eluded him until now.

"I ordered me a Ninja black belt training course from the International Ninja Training Academy for two hundred dollars. It took all my savings, but it'll be worth it. And they included the uniform for free!"

"That so?" Sarge grunted.

"Yes Sir."

"After I complete six lessons and send them in to Master Nu, he'll send me my Black Belt and official Certificate of Graduation."

Although Sarge showed little hint of his approval or disapproval of Teddy's venture, his eyes smiled ever so slightly in response to Teddy's excitement.

"Teddy, why do you want to become a Ninja?"

Without hesitation, Teddy revealed his plan: "The thing about being a Ninja is that they teach you how to be invisible— you know—in a good way. You can sneak around, and even though people won't know you're there, you can be on the look-out."

"Look-out for what?" Sarge asked.

"Look-out for any danger that might come their way so you can rescue them," Teddy replied. "Your identity stays a secret. It's like you're a secret hero helping out people in trouble. Nobody might ever know the good you do, but at least you'll know. I'm gonna be like the invisible protector of Muskgrove Lane."

Sarge looked at Teddy and smiled. "Well Teddy, all I can tell you is that I'm glad there'll be a Ninja looking out for me in Muskgrove Lane."

That said, he picked up his basketball and began to walk toward home. Looking over his shoulder, he shouted, "See you boys next Saturday."

As the years passed, Muskgrove Lane, like all neighborhoods, endured the usual timeworn transformations marked by the end of some things and the beginning of others. Seasons changed, hairlines receded, and graduations brushed shoulders with first-birthday celebrations. Even Jack shed the "Little" from his childhood moniker. On his fifteenth birthday, Little Jack made it clear that henceforth he would be addressed as "Jack." Anyone who referred to him as Little Jack would do so at his or her own peril, which translated into the teenage code of Muskgrove Lane as an "ass whipping." Occasionally adults slipped up and addressed him as Little Jack. When they did, he met their response with a cold stare and a stony silence. Only Teddy who had always been oblivious to neighborhood etiquette and traditions seemed able to get away with calling Jack, "Little Jack."

On a cool autumn afternoon, Sarge spotted Teddy walking in the rain on the shoulder of Highway 87.

Sarge eased his Jeep Cherokee off the highway, rolled down the passenger side window and waited for Teddy.

Within several minutes, Teddy peered in through the open window. "Hi, Sarge."

"Hi, Teddy. How about a ride home?"

"Okay. Thanks," Teddy replied easing himself into the back seat.

Lloyd looked at him in the rearview mirror.

"How's things going?"

Teddy didn't respond right away. "Me and my stepfather ain't getting along too good. Never really have. He don't understand me. Guess it's hard to understand someone you don't much like."

Teddy's eyes met Lloyd's in the rearview mirror, then he looked out into the rain. "I don't know what's gonna happen."

The Jeep Cherokee came to a stop where the gravel road began that led to the house trailer.

Lloyd put the gearshift lever in park and turned to Teddy.

"Teddy, whatever happens, I want you to remember something."

"Remember what, Sarge?"

"That you're a good boy."

"You really think so?"

"I know so, Teddy," Lloyd replied.

The corners of Teddy's mouth curved in the hint of a weary smile. He didn't quite believe what Sarge said, but appreciated the gesture nonetheless.

Getting out of the Jeep, he closed the door and peered through the passenger window. "Thanks for the ride, Sarge."

"Anytime, Teddy."

Lloyd listened to the gravel crunch grinding beneath his wheels as he pulled away from Teddy. He turned his head to look back. He could, just for a moment, barely make out Teddy, climbing his driveway with the heavy uncertain feet of an old man.

Time moved on. Like most people, the residents of Muskgrove Lane were preoccupied with the busyness of their lives—births, funerals, weddings, graduations and everything that went on in between. Jack and the others graduated from high school and then went off to college, work, or wherever else their dreams and fears led them. The basketball court in the cul-de-sac looked lonely, having to settle for sporadic contests of "Horse" or "21." The glory days were gone and like all holiday seasons, Detective Lloyd Burns was overworked and underpaid.

Staring out of his office window and finishing the last of his stale, lukewarm cup of coffee, Lloyd watched the snowflakes float by in the dusk of evening. For police officers and detectives, Christmas wasn't particularly merry. When the phone rang at the precinct station, it wasn't to announce that Santa was passing out gifts, but more likely that he was passed out in an alleyway downtown. For the men and women of Precinct 44, Christmas was a time of drunken domestic squabbles, traffic accidents initiated by harried, preoccupied last-minute shoppers, and barroom brawls where patrons, not reindeer, sported red noses. Lloyd chuckled softly to himself. "Tis the season to be jolly."

"Hey, Lloyd, Officer Klein wants to see you down at Intake," roared McGillicutty, the burly Desk Sergeant.

"What does she want?"

McGillicutty looked up from the mound of paperwork on his desk and scowled. "Hell, if I know. What do I look like, a damn encyclopedia!"

Lloyd Burns looked at the clock. Ten minutes to quitting time. He grabbed his briefcase and ambled down the hall to the Intake room where he found Patrol Officer Susan Klein thumbing through a dog-eared card file.

"Susan, what can I do for you this fine evening?"

"Probably nothing. I thought I'd give you a head's up on a young guy we just picked up on a solicitation and drug possession charge down in the 'fresh meat' district. Said he knew you." Lloyd's heart sank.

"What's his name?"

Officer Klein flipped through the paperwork on her desk

"Let's see—here it is. He goes by the name Teddy Runion."

Lloyd took a deep breath. "Yeah, I know him. What's the deal on him?"

Scrutinizing her report, Officer Klein talked as she read.

"Looks like it's his third arrest. Twice for prostitution and once for drugs. He's currently on probation which more than likely will be revoked, and since he's just turned eighteen, he may buy some time." Rubbing his chin, Lloyd stared at Officer Klein.

"How 'bout diversion programs? Teddy was a good kid. Grew up in my neighborhood. He had a tough life—not many breaks."

"Yeah, didn't they all," Klein said as she neatly stacked the arrest reports. "You might try Chris Smith's half-way house over in Chillicowee. He runs a good program. Better than most. A lot of his kids seem to make it."

"Thanks, Klein. I'll check it out. And thanks for the heads up."

"Don't mention it."

Lloyd called his wife as he had done so often before and begged off the Christmas party at her sister's. Having been a police officer's wife for twenty years she understood, but still found it difficult to mask her disappointment. Although he wasn't sure why, Lloyd didn't tell her about Teddy. There would be time enough for that later.

Lloyd spent the next two and a half hours making calls. Two programs turned him down and a third put Teddy's name on a waiting list. Finally, Chris Smith returned his call. Mustering up the last of his day's energy and stopping just short of begging, Lloyd gave Chris his best shot.

There was a long pause on the other end of the line.

"Okay, Detective. It must be the Christmas spirit. I'll find a way to make room for him. Bring him by tomorrow morning."

"Thanks, Chris. I owe you."

"Yes, you do Detective. Yes, you do."

The good news seemed to refresh Lloyd as he sauntered back down to Intake. He allowed himself a small smile and imagined that this could be a life-changing break for Teddy. Lloyd looked through the interview window at Teddy. He had changed. His blond hair was still meticulously combed, but his face had a drawn, gaunt look to it. His left arm sported a tattoo of an angel. Lloyd opened the door and walked inside.

"Sarge!" Teddy exclaimed, standing up and extending his hand.

"Hi, Teddy. Long time, no see."

Teddy rubbed one eye and kept the other fixated on the badge clinging to Lloyd's coat pocket. "It really has been," he said, nodding to intensify his delivery.

"How are you doing?"

Teddy stopped rubbing his eye and smiled. "I've had better days—worse ones too."

Lloyd nodded to an invisible beat and tapped on his coffee cup, his mind scrambling for the right thing to say. "Teddy, you know you don't have to live like this. I have friends who could find you a place at a half-way house. There are drug treatment center options, counseling— anything you need."

Teddy's face softened, his eyes a little less shaded.

"Sarge, I really appreciate you trying to help me, but the truth is, I don't want to change."

Lloyd leaned in closer. "You sure? Because I really want to—I really do know some folks who can help you."

Teddy's face looked older, lines and creases sculpted by long walks up a gravel driveway.

"Yeah, Sarge," he said, "I'm sure."

Lloyd Burns tried, but couldn't hide his disappointment. He felt like he had been punctured with a giant pin and all the air had been sucked out of him. He tried to give Teddy a smile, but only partially succeeded, so instead, he patted him on the shoulder and motioned to Officer Klein that he was through.

As she led Teddy out of the office, he turned and looked at the Detective. "Hey Sarge, you remember that time you gave me a ride home in the rain?"

Lloyd looked up and nodded his head.

"You said I was a good boy. I never forgot that."

Sitting in silence, Lloyd cradled his coffee cup in his palm and watched Teddy disappear down the hallway.

9   *Rasheed's Ticket*

The green vinyl sofa squeaked as Rasheed Smith shifted his weight in Mel Evans' office. Evans responded to the noise by casting an involuntary glance in the young man's direction and then refocused his attention on the inmate's folder and written request.

As Evans studied Rasheed's file, Rasheed examined the details of the caseworker's office for the umpteenth time while a small oscillating fan did its best to dispel the humidity of a mid-western summer. An orange shag carpet, Jimi Hendrix poster, over-sized boom box and lava lamp were the predominant features of Mel Evans' work environment, or as he liked to refer to it, his "pad." Rasheed wondered to himself what the caseworker's real home must look like. Was it as funky as his office?

Two things were common knowledge among the brothers in the cellblock: first that Mr. Evans for one reason or another was lost in the sixties and seventies, and second, that he wanted to be accepted by black inmates. It was primarily the second reason that Rasheed had come to him with this particular request.

Mel Evans quietly folded the file and placed it upon the desk as Rasheed gazed absent-mindedly at the picture of Jimi Hendrix.

Evans smiled. "No one played guitar like Jimi. I'm convinced that 'All along the Watchtower' is the greatest rock song ever recorded."

Rasheed nodded. "Yes Sir, except that he didn't write it."

"What's that?"

"He didn't write it. Bob Dylan did."

"I had no idea. That's some Hendrix trivia lost on me. But you're right, he was something else with that guitar. Damn straight he was," Evans continued as he launched into his well-known version of how black music, from slave-inspired spirituals to current rap and hip-hop, had shaped and enriched the musical landscape of American culture.

Rasheed sighed and did as countless other inmates of color had done, trying his best to appear interested in the caseworker's timeworn soliloquy.

Satisfied that he had duly impressed Rasheed with his empathy and understanding of minorities, Mel Evans folded his hands and placed them on his desktop.

"First, Rasheed let me say that I'm really impressed with your progress. Last year, you had six write-ups for fighting. This year you only had one. And here you are graduating at the top of your class. Out of 21 student residents, you have the highest grade-point average. I can't tell you how proud I am of you."

"Thank you, Sir."

"While your request is out of the ordinary, I can certainly understand why you would want your momma to share your graduation experience with you."

Rasheed broke into a smile. "Yes Sir. She ain't never seen nothin' but trouble with me. This would show her another side. It would mean a lot to her and to me and . . ."

Caseworker Evans interrupted Rasheed in mid-sentence. "I know it would. And I would love to help out. I really would. Trouble is I don't have any funds or resources to help you get her here for the ceremony. I'm really sorry I can't help."

"Not even for a bus ticket?" Rasheed countered. "She could stay with her sister in Lincoln. All she would need is a round-trip bus ticket."

Evans' silence accentuated Rasheed's disappointment.

"Tell you what; let me check with Chaplin Stinson. I know he has a small rainy-day fund for special needs. Maybe he can help you and your momma out. Why don't you make an appointment with him next week? I'll put in a good word for you."

A hint of hope returned as Rasheed shook hands with the caseworker.

Corporal Smitty Hudson scooped a fresh pinch of Skoal from the round tin and placed it under his tongue as he watched Rasheed close the caseworker's door behind him. He had never really liked the young man walking toward him. On more than one occasion, Rasheed had been a real pain in the ass. And besides he was black. Smitty's Granddaddy had believed in segregation. Even two generations removed, after a racial incident in his cell house, he would find himself reconsidering the wisdom of his Granddaddy's conviction.

"You ready to head back to your kitchen work assignment?"

"Yes Sir," Rasheed replied as he fell into step with the older man's slow walk.

"Evans' still got that picture of that hippie guitar player on his wall and that orange rug?"

"Yes Sir."

Corporal Hudson chuckled to himself and spit a stream of tobacco juice into the styrofoam cup he carried in his right hand.

"That boy is a piece of work."

Talking to himself as much as to the Corporal, Rasheed responded, "That he is, Sir. That he is."

Chaplain Stinson was an earnest sort of man. A Methodist minister, he had pastored two small churches in Oklahoma before he was hired as Senior Chaplain for the State Prison. Although the title did appeal to him, he was well aware that he was not only the senior Chaplain, but also the only Chaplain serving over 2000 resident inmates in a prison originally built for 1200. He was grateful for the Catholic and Lutheran volunteer Chaplains and tolerant of the Muslim Cleric who held services once a month in the gym.

Chaplain Stinson's office was as calm and simple as Mel Evans' office was loud and gaudy. He personally found the institutional pale green color of his office and the chapel serene. A large bronze crucifix hung on the wall behind his desk. The Chaplain cared about the inmates in his charge in a serious, yet distant, sort of way. At the monthly meetings of the local ministerial association, he was fond of referring to the inmate residents at the state prison as his "errant flock."

Other than a desk, an executive chair, and a computer hutch, the only other furniture was a single chair for visitors, positioned directly in front of his desk. Chaplain Stinson's office had a neat and austere look to it. There was in fact, a sense of order and authority. During last year's annual private retreat, Fred Stinson had experienced an epiphany. In the midst of the chaos of prison life and all the anguish and darkness the residents brought with them, his office and chapel were to be an oasis of clarity and certainty. While the authority of the criminal justice system had placed the residents in the State Prison, it was the higher authority— the Supreme Judge— that constituted his domain of concern. As he like to put it, he was not only concerned with correcting their misbehavior, but with their "eternal rehabilitation" as well. Sipping the steaming cup of Earl Grey tea, Chaplain Stinson carefully perused Rasheed Smith's file and written request. The young man had certainly made progress. There was no doubt about that. From aggression in the cell house to aggressively pursuing his education—it was an excellent example of sublimation. The Chaplain smiled to himself. His continuing studies in psychoanalysis were bearing fruit. His personal reflections were interrupted by Jerry, his inmate assistant.

"Chaplain, your three o'clock is here."

"Excellent, Jerry, send him in."

After Rasheed had seated himself, the Chaplain quietly observed him for several moments before he spoke.

"I've read your request and reviewed your file, Rasheed. And I must say I am impressed with the progress you have made."

"Yes Sir. Thank you, Sir," Rasheed responded with a mix of hope and consternation. "It's just that my momma ain't never seen this side of me. She only seen what I was in the past— the bad part of me. She's scraped together all the money she can get her hands on and she can stay with her sister in Lincoln—so all she needs is fifty-five dollars to help pay for the bus ticket. Mr. Evans said you had a special fund that might be able to help my momma to get to my graduation."

Chaplain Stinson folded his hands together and looked at Rasheed intently.

"It is true that I have access to a 'special needs' fund. Unfortunately, the balance of that account has been earmarked to handle expenses associated with the spring concert of the Singspirations. The men have been practicing all year and the townfolk always give a generous love offering at the end of the concert. Those donations are essential to our Chapel music program. So, as much as I would like to help you and your mother, Rasheed, it wouldn't be fair to the choir members or townspeople. I'm truly sorry."

Rasheed said nothing. His disappointment was obvious. He could feel the anger of the "old" Rasheed boiling up in his belly as he rose to leave.

"Wait a minute, young man. Before you go, let's have a word of prayer. Tell you what, we will pray for a miracle. You know, God's in the miracle business!"

Rasheed bit his lip. "That's alright Chaplain, I don't really feel . . ."

"I insist!" Chaplain Stinson interrupted."

The Chaplain waxed eloquent for a few moments about miracles and faith and such while Rasheed bowed his head and counted the tiny colored squares on the rug beneath his feet in an effort to keep his composure.

Like before, Corporal Hudson was waiting to escort Rasheed back to the kitchen. As they walked down the long corridor, the correctional officer leisurely worked the toothpick between his teeth. "Those hamburgers at lunch had a lot of gristle in them."

Rasheed said nothing, counting the green floor tiles as the two of them proceeded toward their destination.

"Strike out again?"

"Struck out again," Rasheed whispered.

Hudson retrieved the toothpick from his mouth and pushed it into his shirt pocket for later use.

"Well, one thing's for sure. Getting a piece of paper with a high school diploma on it is a sight better than all papers you got with write-ups on 'em. And I ought to know cause I signed quite a few myself." "Guess so," Rasheed murmured to no one in particular.

The keynote speaker for graduation day was the local high school principal who delivered an inspiring, if somewhat awkward "grand accomplishments and new horizons" kind of message. The 21 graduates and their family members sat in metal folding chairs in the educational annex for the duration of the ceremony. The day was hot and the participants sweated together in a sea of smiles and pride.

Dressed in cap and gown, Rasheed was grinning from ear to ear as he received a plaque and special medallion for graduating first in his class.

After the ceremony, the reception tables beckoned the graduates, family members, and attending staff with sandwiches, cookies and punch, courtesy of the prison kitchen workers. There was even a special cake honoring one of their own, Rasheed, for his accomplishment.

As everyone circled around the tables, Rasheed insisted that his momma help him cut the first piece of cake while her sister, Verona, took their picture. That photograph would become the most valued of personal artifacts belonging to Rasheed—a reminder of something positive to build his life around, a sign of possibilities, the hope of better times to come.

All the prison dignitaries were there. The Superintendent figured if he was going to show up and shake hands, so would every other professional who worked in the prison that he deemed relevant to such a high event. Caseworker Evans and Chaplain Stinson were among those professionals so identified. They stood among graduates and family members, smiling, sipping their punch and doing their duty.

Chaplain Stinson was especially pleased to see that Rasheed's mother was able to attend her son's graduation.

As Rasheed prepared to refill his momma's cup with punch, the Chaplain called out to him.

"Rasheed."

Rasheed turned to the approaching Chaplain.

"Congratulations, son. I am so pleased that your   mother was able to attend the ceremony."

"Yes Sir," Rasheed responded while refilling his momma's cup.

"Remember our prayer that day in my office when everything looked so bleak? Events have a way of working out when we give God the credit and rely on his will. I believe your mother's presence here today is proof of that. Miracles can still happen. With God, the impossible becomes possible."

Rasheed's smile disappeared. He quietly looked at Chaplain Stinson before he spoke.

"Can't say much about miracles or what God had to do with it, but I guess I'd have to give any credit that was due to Corporal Hudson."

"Corporal Hudson?"

"Yeah, it was the Corporal who sent my momma the bus ticket. He never said nothin' to me 'bout it. 'Course I thanked him when my momma wrote me."

The Chaplain was clearly surprised. "I wonder why he did it? Of course, it's wonderful that he did."

"Don't know. Me and the Corporal never got along that well. Guess you'd have to ask him," Rasheed replied as he gathered up a chocolate chip cookie to go with the punch.

Smitty Hudson knocked on Chaplain Stinson's office door. He had come to retrieve a young inmate who had been placed on suicide watch.

The Chaplain opened the door and instructed the young inmate he had been counseling to wait in the reception area while he had a word with the Corporal.

Corporal Hudson closed the door behind him.

"What can I do for you Chaplain?"

"Smitty, I wanted to tell you how impressed I am regarding your gesture of generosity concerning Rasheed and his mother last week."

Corporal Hudson shrugged, "Nothing to be impressed about."

"I beg to differ," the Chaplain replied. "But I must confess to some curiosity as to why you helped out? As I recall, Rasheed gave you a great deal of trouble last year. I believe I remember that he even took a swing at you on an occasion when you were trying to break up a fight."

"Truth is, he took two swings, not one. He missed with the first one, but I caught a black eye with the second."

Chaplain Stinson smiled, amazed. "And yet, with all the trouble he caused you, you still helped him."

"Don't understand the fuss, Chaplain. Rasheed's done some bad things in his life. May do some more. But his schooling's a good thing that also took some doing."

"Still, the bus ticket for his mother came out of your own pocket," the Chaplain said. "That's certainly going the extra mile. What was your inspiration for such an impressive act of generosity?"

Smitty Hudson looked at the Chaplain as though he was confused.

"Can't say as I'm getting your point. Like I said, the boy who was doing bad, done good. And his momma deserved to see the good. Don't know about no extra mile or inspiration. What I do know is it's almost quittin' time and I got to get that inmate back to the medical section."

Smitty turned to retrieve his charge. "See you later, Chaplain."

10 *The Mercy Seat*

"That's right, Jethro. Day after tomorrow, you'll be ridin' that roller-coaster straight to hell!" Elroy Perkins shouted, raising his voice like an old-time evangelist preaching his last night at a dirt-road revival. "And it'll be one hot ride." Of course, Elroy was no evangelist. He was the kind of man who made sport of disabled children and prison rape victims, and had no idea what joy or happiness felt like. The closest Elroy could come was to experience a kind of perverted pleasure in response to the pain and suffering of others, and the most genuine smile he could muster always ended up looking like a sneer.

The object of Elroy's tirade responded with a series of low moans and muffled sobs. Jethro curled up on his prison cot and tried to block out the taunts, but like all the other times, the ridicule seeped through the fingers that covered his ears and touched the fear deep within him. Elroy had his number.

"Jethro's" real name was Gerald. He was from the red clay hill country of North Georgia. Twenty-six years old and a petty criminal since he was fourteen, Gerald had been housed in Section D of the Row for a little over seven years. His most recent incarceration was the result of an incident involving him and his two older cousins, Alvin and Earl. During a night of drinking and big talk, they had come upon a high-school couple having a romantic interlude in the back seat of a Ford Taurus on Hollow Leg Ridge. With the boldness that only alcohol can provide, Gerald and his cousins robbed the couple. When the boy, Lester Johnson, an All-State tight end for the local high school, resisted, they killed him and raped his girlfriend, Wanda Jean, leaving her naked and delirious on a frigid October night. Gerald was the only one who received the death sentence, compliments of his cousins turning state's evidence and the inadequacy of his court appointed attorney.

If the truth were known, Gerald was a follower, not a leader. He never initiated anything, but was always ready to go along for the ride, and more often than not, as evidenced by his numerous juvenile court appearances, rarely knew where the ride was going. In fact, on the night in question, Gerald wet his pants at the sight of Wanda Jean being sexually assaulted by his cousins. He remained a virgin, although no one, especially the jury, believed him. Someone had to pay for the death of Lester and the rape of Wanda Jean, and Alvin and Earl decided to elect Gerald. Barely able to read and burdened with an unmistakable hillbilly accent, Gerald had been renamed Jethro by his twelve fellow boarders on Section D of death row at the State Prison. Day after tomorrow, he was going to take a final ride, as Elroy had so cruelly put it. And for once, he knew where the ride was going.

Elroy was Jethro's chief tormenter on death row. Although Elroy was his birth name, he hated it. He wished his name was Elvis, like the King of Rock and Roll. Elroy saw himself as a ladies' man and a general all-around bad boy. He often addressed other men not by their given name but by the term "Honcho," or "*Cacaos*," or "Chief." And Elroy was more than a little proud of the crude tattoo scrawled the length of his left forearm. It read "Bad to the Bone," and few who knew him would disagree.

He had previously served twelve years in prison for beating to death the man who had taken up with his former girlfriend. Three days after he was released from prison, he killed his ex-girlfriend and was sentenced to death. He had bragged before and after he killed her that "No woman leaves Elroy T. Perkins and lives to talk about it." Of course, many had throughout Elroy's life, starting with his mother, Eunice, when he was six years old.

There had been other assaults, physical and sexual, in Elroy's past that he had not been charged with—usually due to intimidation and on occasion, dumb luck. Elroy's Grandmother had raised him and had been heard to say on more than one occasion that Elroy himself was, more or less, an assault on the human race. Her words turned out to be prophetic. Elroy rarely passed on an opportunity to insult or harass anyone he came in contact with. When he wasn't targeting other inmates or the occasional correctional officer for abuse, he lay on his cot and sulked. While the other inmates had backed off hassling Jethro, who on a good day was an easy target for ridicule and laughter, Elroy, instead, turned up the heat.

When a death row inmate was nearing his execution date, a strange kind of solidarity encompassed his death row compatriots. Even occasional words of encouragement could be heard coming from one cell or another in the long, hot nights leading up the designated man's final walk. It was a reverent, unspoken tradition on death row, a kind of "don't speak ill of the one who is about to be dead." Of course, Elroy didn't observe traditions, especially ones that deprived him of the simple pleasures found in tormenting the doomed and the damned.

Lost in his own thoughts, a middle-aged man with a slight paunch and graying temples, turned from the small window he was looking through, and faced his night shift partner, Officer Ed Jenkins, who was clearly agitated.

"The boy's carrying-on is unsettling the other men. Things are getting a little dicey. You think we ought to try to put a lid on that asshole Elroy and maybe calm the kid down? The Doc's done given him all the 'meds' he's gonna get until tomorrow."

Popping a fresh stick of chewing gum in his mouth, he looked at Ed Jenkins and replied, "I'll see what I can do."

That's really how it all started. Up until that moment, Cleve Jefferson, known by many as Bishop, was just another inmate waiting on death in Section D.

Although most men on any death row are usually low-keyed to the point of being docile, there is always one or two Elroy's to contend with. Sometimes the troublemakers are mentally ill, but there are others like Elroy who are just plain mean. Of course, the former doesn't necessarily exclude the latter. One could be both mean and crazy.

The only way to deal with a primitive like Elroy was to make clear to him that the pain you were going to cause him was substantially greater than the pleasure he was experiencing. For Elroy, it was the threat of having his one hour a day on the small, interior exercise yard taken from him. To make sure he got the point, Sergeant J.T. Jones added the possibility that his canteen privileges would be suspended for a month. The threat of no Cokes, candy, or Little Debby snack cakes drove Elroy pouting to his cot in the corner of his cell.

Elroy's bullshit was contained in short order. Jethro's fragile grasp on reality proved to be another matter. What Elroy had put in motion seemed to have taken on a life of its own as Jethro's moans turned to wailing and left him curled up in a fetal position on the floor of his cell. Ed Jenkins was getting more than a little concerned. "What are we gonna do, Sarge?"

"I'm not sure, Ed," J.T. answered. "One thing I do know is that if we wake Major Dawson from his evening nap at Central Control, there will be hell to pay. I think I'll take one more shot at trying to calm him down."

J.T. Jones tried to talk to Jethro in his most soothing voice, but his crying intensified and brought curses and shouts for quiet from the other inmates who were trying to sleep.

"All right son," J.T. said to himself as much as anyone else. "I guess I'll go wake up the Major."

As he walked down the corridor to his office, a voice called out to him from cell 11. "Sergeant Jones."

J.T. stopped and walked back to Bishop's cell.

A small, bald black man with long, gray sideburns looked at him intently. "I believe I could help the young man."

"And how would you do that?" J.T. asked, scratching his left ear.

"Me and him been talking a lot the last few days.

I've been praying for him and I believe he might listen to me."

"Thanks for your offer, Bishop, but I doubt Jethro would listen to anybody in his present state. And with what's facing him day after tomorrow, I can't say as I blame him. Anyway, you're three cells down from him—not close enough to carry on much of a conversation."

Bishop sat down on his cot and smiled.

"Sergeant, I can't help you with the cell arrangements, but I can help you with Gerald."

J.T. looked at Bishop for a moment, then shook his head and walked back to his office.

"Good God! You can't be serious," Ed exclaimed. "We could be fired!"

"Not if you keep your mouth shut," J.T. replied, popping a fresh stick of gum in his mouth.

"If anything goes wrong, I'll take the blame."

"Damn straight you will!" Ed responded. "If the shit hits the fan, I'm deaf, dumb, and blind."

As J.T. unlocked Bishop's cell door, he was amused that Bishop didn't seem to be surprised by his actions. With his tattered Bible in hand, Bishop proceeded to the chair J.T. had placed next to the condemned man's cell.

J.T. positioned himself where he could maintain a clear vision, while allowing Bishop and Jethro some measure of privacy. As Bishop pressed his face against the bars of Jethro's cell door, J.T. clearly heard only one word during his thirty-minute vigil.

"Gerald."

Even after all these years, J.T. was still amazed at the effect that one word had on the delirious young man. At the single utterance of his name, Jethro's body relaxed and he grew silent. Bishop said nothing, but sat and waited. From his vantage point J.T. could see Jethro sit up within a few minutes of Bishop's greeting and crawl on his hands and knees toward the small, black man with the long gray sideburns. What followed were whispers that sounded like praying. First Bishop, then Jethro. Then Bishop passed his Bible through the bars to the young prisoner and they clasped hands in silence, simply looking at each other for a time. Finally, Bishop smiled at Jethro, rose to his feet and walked back to the front of his cell. Once J.T. had locked the door behind him, Bishop turned and looked at him with quiet approval.

"Thank you, Sergeant Jones."

Nodding his head, J.T. went to check on Jethro and found him curled up on his cot, his face pressed against Bishop's Bible. Jethro looked up at the Sergeant for a brief moment, but said nothing and then closed his eyes.

Walking back to the office, Sergeant J.T. Jones experienced a strange sensation. He felt light-headed. Jethro's look had unsettled him, and he had the strange feeling that on that particular night it was Bishop, and not him, who was in control of his domain. J.T. was grateful for the steaming cup of coffee Ed offered him.

Two days later, Jethro was executed.

Cleve Jefferson, who came to be known on death row as "Bishop," never denied his guilt. He had been a small-time drug dealer who killed two rivals in a shoot-out. That act alone would not have put him on death row even with the list of other crimes and drug related assaults on his rap sheet. Cleve's ticket to death row came as a result of his accidentally shooting Maria Lopez, a single mother with two young children during the same shoot-out.

During his first two years on the row, he had been an angry young man, ranting against a racist justice system and filing endless appeals. Then one day, without explanation, Cleve Jefferson gradually became less belligerent and less talkative. As he began to withdraw, Doc Hansen assumed he was experiencing the kind of depression typical for death row inmates and offered him anti-depressants, which he politely refused. Soon after, he quit talking altogether.

For six months, Cleve Jefferson said nothing. He slept, ate and sat on the edge of his cot, staring at the picture of Maria Lopez he had torn out of a newspaper. From time to time deep in the night, sobbing could be heard coming from his cell. Correctional officers on all three shifts pooled their money to see who would correctly guess the night Cleve Jefferson would take his life.

On New Year's Day of his third year on death row, Cleve Jefferson began to talk again. Over the next two years, he collected and read a variety of religious and holy books, including the Bible, the Koran, the Ramayana, the Tao Te Ching, the Tibetan Book of the Dead and Black Elk Speaks. Although Cleve seemed to prefer the Bible or his "Grandmama's Book" as he referred to it, he read and studied a wide variety of religious and wisdom traditions. He also began to share his readings and thoughts with anyone on the row who would listen. Most didn't, but a few did. Those few seemed intrigued with what he had to say and began to refer to Cleve as "Bishop." Over the years, everyone—officer and inmate alike—came to refer to him as Bishop as much out of habit as anything else. Most of the officers figured Cleve had gone a little crazy but accepted that the men on death row coped with their predicament in different ways as best they could.

The only non-inmate who would talk with Cleve about spiritual matters was a good-natured young Chaplain who seemed to genuinely enjoy their conversations. His two favorite expressions to Bishop were "I go to three years of Seminary to become a Reverend and you go to death row and end up a Bishop" and "I'll convert you to a Baptist yet." Each time Chaplain Smith would utter either of those phrases, Bishop's response was always the same—a smile and a chuckle. Bishop had been on death row for ten years when he thanked Sergeant J.T. Jones for letting him talk to Jethro. After that night, everything changed.

At first, their chats would last only ten or fifteen minutes, usually in the wee hours of the morning while the other inmates were asleep and Ed Jenkins was doing paperwork. Gradually, fifteen-minute chats evolved into two-hour conversations between two men, separated by prison bars, race, and a lifetime of different experiences. Their conversations ranged from prison life to sports to religion or whatever else caught their fancy. J.T. would sit in a folding chair with his coffee cup and thermos and Bishop on the edge of his cot, finishing the last of the sweet potato pie J.T. had slipped him, compliments of Margie, J.T.'s wife of twenty years.

J.T. Jones was not a particularly sentimental man. He honored the obligatory birthdays and other holidays with friendly resolve. He wasn't against such occasions any more than he was against going to the Methodist church with his wife on most Sunday mornings. Such traditions just didn't hold much appeal for him. J.T. seemed to find more solace walking in the woods on the farm that had been his Daddy's before it was his and his Granddaddy's before that. Only the occasional bird in flight could hear him singing the hymns of his youth while he pole-fished from the banks of the old mill pond on the back side of his farm.

It wasn't so much that J.T. Jones was a simple man, but more that his needs and wants were simple. He had driven the same pickup truck for the last twelve years and for the most part, lived his life from the inside out. He was a careful and practical man who was at the same time, curious in a quiet sort of a way. And when a situation called for it, he was willing to go against convention and take a chance. It was a mix of the three—curiosity, inwardness and non-conformity that drew J.T. to Bishop.

J.T.'s practical and careful nature required that he first review the file and background of the man who had come to be known as Bishop. The conclusion had been clear. Cleve Jefferson had become Bishop through some sort of gradual transformation, which in itself was not that uncommon on death row. J.T. had witnessed a number of men experience genuine religious conversions when facing death. Getting one's house in order, seeking some sense of forgiveness for the harm that one has done, and looking for hope in a better life beyond the grave—a fresh start so to speak—were understandable to J.T. What was different about Bishop in contrast to the others was that he didn't seem to follow any particular tradition. He didn't claim to be a Baptist, Methodist, Catholic, or Muslim. All J.T. ever heard him refer to himself as when he conversed with other inmates, was that he was one of "God's boys." In fact, every morning, seven days a week, when breakfast was served,

Bishop always issued forth the same greeting to the residents of death row, Section D: "How are God's boys this morning?"

The responses to his daily query were varied and ranged from silence to complimentary replies, and on occasion, expletive-laced retorts from inmates like Elroy. J.T. smiled as he recalled a particular breakfast exchange between Bishop and Elroy, who had awakened in a particularly foul mood.

"Damn God's boys and damn you, you no-account Nigger!" snarled Elroy. "You were born a Nigger and you'll die a Nigger. A Nigger is all you'll ever be."

After the course of profanities subsided, which echoed from other inmates toward Elroy, Bishop simply chuckled and responded in a clear, calm voice: "You're more right than you know, Elroy. I was a Nigger just as you are. We're all Niggers until we sit in the mercy seat. It's only through the mercy seat that Niggers like you and me can become men in this world and children of God."

Of course, Elroy didn't agree with Bishop's assessment and let him know in no uncertain terms before returning to his cot.

Eventually, the residents of Section D seemed to look forward to rather than tolerate Bishop's early morning greeting. J.T. and the other officers began to sense a kind of respect and even affection on the part of the other inmates toward the old man.

Numerous helpings of sweet potato pie, cooked greens and homemade cornbread later, J.T. Jones finally got around to asking Bishop the questions he had been curious about for a long time.

Handing Bishop a fresh cup of coffee through the bars, J.T. paused before he spoke.

"Bishop, exactly what kind of religious man are you? You say you are one of God's boys, but what does that mean? You got all these books about different religions and such, but you've never said what your religion is—only that you are one of God's boys." J.T. stopped talking and took a long sip of his coffee.

"That's a pretty long question, Sergeant. Anything else?"

"Yeah, what's the 'mercy seat'?" J.T. asked, warming his hands on his coffee cup.

Bishop closed his eyes and sat quietly before answering. Finally, he spoke.

"I've read, prayed and meditated on the holy books of many faiths. The reason I keep coming back to the Bible is because it's my Grandmama's book. She called it the 'Good Book.' To me, it's 'Grandmama's Book.' You know, she raised me for the first eight years of my life, before she died of the consumption. Sitting on her front porch in the late afternoon after she had returned from working in the fields, we would drink mason jars filled with strong, sweet tea. Every afternoon, my Grandmama would read to me from the 'Good Book' and tell me stories about Jesus and the Holy Ghost. Sometimes her stories would lift me up beyond the clouds and other times they'd scare the pure hell out of me. She was a small woman with a big faith I didn't understand at the time." Bishop paused to take a sip of coffee.

"After all my praying, reading and studying, I can't really say I know all that much 'bout anything. What I can say is that I love the Jesus my Grandmama taught me about. I guess you could say that I think of myself as a 'Jesus Man' who has a lot of friends and relatives from other faith traditions. Chaplain Smith, of course, doesn't agree," Bishop said, chuckling. "He says all my friends and relatives are going straight to hell." Bishop drank the last of his coffee and smiled. "I like him. He's a young man with good intentions and a lot of back roads left to travel." J.T. refilled Bishop's cup with coffee from his thermos.

"Tell me about the 'mercy seat.'"

Bishop closed his eyes once again and grew quiet. J.T. sipped his coffee in silence and waited.

"When I was dealing drugs, violence was a way of life— nothing special. Intimidation, beatings and sexual assaults, even murder—nothing special. And then the shooting—nothing new, except this time, I killed a single mother in the crossfire. Left two small children behind. I'd seen innocent people hurt—even killed, but never by my hand."

"From the time I saw her picture at the trial, I became affected in a way that's hard to explain. It's like I was haunted. I cut that dead woman's picture out of the newspaper and carried it with me. At night, I'd dream that my Grandmama was looking at me, tears streaming from her eyes. During the day, I found myself either looking at the picture of the woman that I killed or thinking about her two children."

"When I arrived here on death row, I taped Maria Lopez's picture on the wall at the end of my cot. Then I wrote my cousin, Angela, and asked her to send me my Grandmama's Bible. Felt like I was going crazy, staring at that picture of Maria Lopez all day and dreaming about my Grandmama all night."

"When my Grandmama's 'Good Book' came in the mail, things began to change. As I began to read and to pray, I stopped dreaming about her. Then I quit talking and ate very little."

J.T. interjected, "We thought you were losing it—had you on 24-hour suicide watch."

"All I was concerned about was the picture on my wall and the hot ball of pain that was filling up my insides. I felt like I couldn't breathe . . . felt like I was on fire. And then one night while I was looking at that photograph, that ball of fire exploded and buried me alive in its ashes."

A thin bead of sweat broke out on Bishop's forehead.

"I felt her suffering as she drew her last breath. I felt the sorrow of her children losing their mother. I felt the loss of her parents and friends. I even felt the pain of my own mama abandoning me when I was a little boy. It was like I was responsible for everything bad that had happened to anybody and everybody. I couldn't bear it. I was drowning in a sea of sorrow. After there were no tears left for me to cry, I began to pray to the Lord Almighty for forgiveness, for deliverance from who I was and what I had become. Then the big change happened."

Bishop grew quiet once more as his eyes filled with tears. J.T. inquired softly, "What was the big change?"

In a choked voice, Bishop replied, "I finally got to sit in the 'mercy seat.' I was crying, praying, meditating and looking at that picture. I don't know how long I had been at it. I had no sense of time—it was like I was outside of time. All I know is what happened next."

"As I looked at that picture, the face of Maria Lopez began to change. Her face began to change into the face of a person I had never seen before. But I knew who it was. It was in the eyes. Not like the pictures on those funeral parlor fans. Different, like peeling off the skin to see what it hid. I been mistaking the rind for the fruit. Those eyes were the fruit—what's behind the behind. It was Him.

I wanted to look away, but I couldn't. Kept looking at that picture for I don't know how long. Then it changed back . . . changed back to the face of the woman I killed. That picture was like a magnet. Couldn't take my eyes off it. And then . . . Oh Lord . . . and then the picture spoke to me. Maria Lopez's picture spoke to me." Once again, Bishop fell silent, his head bowed.

"What did it say?" J.T. asked in a hushed tone.

Bishop looked at J.T. a long time before speaking. "She said, 'I died so that you might live.'"

Neither man spoke for a long time, each lost in his own thoughts.

Finally, Bishop took a deep breath and dried his eyes with the back of his hand. "The mercy seat is about second chances—about being forgiven when forgiveness isn't possible. Having your heart broken into a thousand pieces, then opened up and made new again."

"You got any of that coffee left?" Bishop asked with a weary smile.

Taking a swallow, he continued. "If I've learned one thing from what I experienced, it's that I don't know much of anything. But thank the Lord, I do know about the mercy seat."

Bishop's appeals finally ran out. He had plenty of letters of support, including one from J.T. and Chaplain Smith. They weren't asking for the moon, just that his sentence be commuted to life without parole, but it was an election year and everyone knows that mercy takes a back seat on election years.

The morning Bishop was transferred to the deathwatch cell, J.T. came in even though it was his day off. He came in to say good-bye. It was the last time they sat together, he in his folding chair and Bishop on the edge of his cot.

Bishop looked at him and smiled. "J.T., I guess this is it. It's all she wrote for this old world."

No inmate before or since ever called J.T. by his first name, but on that morning, Bishop did, and to J.T., it seemed only natural. All he could say in response was, "I guess so."

He often wished his response had been more helpful, more encouraging, but that's all J.T. said, "I guess so."

Bishop had a final request for him, a special favor to ask. He wanted J.T. to make a promise to him.

"Promise me something."

"Promise you what?"

Reaching through the bars, Bishop gently placed his right hand on J.T.'s heart. "Promise me you'll remember that you're also one of God's boys."

J.T. couldn't speak. All he could do was nod his head.

After Bishop's death, J.T. received a package from Angela, Bishop's cousin. She wrote in a short note that Bishop had wanted him to have his Grandmama's "Good Book."

Sitting on his front porch, he looked at the book in his lap and smelled the supper Margie was cooking.

Opening the front screen door, Margie peered out at her husband. "Honey, what you thinking about?"

"I'm thinking about this book—and that I'm grateful for you and the life I've had. But as grateful as I am, one thing is as certain as the sun setting over that grove of poplar trees. I miss my friend.

11   *The Open Door*

Just about everyone called my grandfather "Pappa Jim," although I'm not sure why. Pappa Jim and his father were both born and raised in the sleepy farming community of Ashton. My mother, who was his and Grandmama's middle child, said it was because he was kind and helpful to everyone, which was for the most part true. He was always giving away garden vegetables to neighbors and strangers alike. When a barn burned, Pappa Jim would be the first one to show up with his toolbox in hand—even if the barn happened to belong to old man Stringfellow. Stringfellow (or "String-along," as he was known by the locals) once sold a tractor he had promised Pappa Jim to someone else because the man in question had offered him five dollars more. I remember asking him why he would help somebody who had treated him so badly. Amused, he sized up my ten-year-old indignation and chuckled.

"Stringfellow's kind needs our help the most. Maybe if he gets enough help with whatever's been sticking in his craw all these years, he'll come to realize that there's more satisfaction in helping somebody than taking advantage of them."

I can't say that my young boy's logic agreed with the wisdom of my grandfather, but that was the way he was. Pappa Jim didn't hold grudges. He forgave others their faults as easily as he seemed to forget his own shortcomings.

One afternoon, when I asked my dad why he thought everyone referred to my grandfather as Pappa Jim, he thought for several minutes before responding. Lighting his pipe and exhaling a lazy curl of smoke, he concluded it must be because of Pappa

Jim's sense of humor, and that he was a natural storyteller. He had a joke or funny anecdote for every occasion and often brought a smile to even the dourest acquaintance. When Pappa Jim told a story people seemed to laugh in spite of themselves.

I asked Grandmama the same question. She looked at me, threw her head back and laughed. "Child, you are something. Now go get yourself one of those sugar cookies while I pour you a glass of milk."

It was always like that. Food was the currency of Grandmama's conversations and her response to most queries. I never did figure out why everyone called my Grandfather Pappa Jim. I came to believe it was because he looked and acted like the grandfather everyone secretly wished they had. Although everyone called me Jamie, my real name was Jim, just like his. I was proud to be named after him. He was my best friend. We had our disagreements from time to time, but like best friends usually do, we always made up in short order. Pappa Jim taught me to work and play. The hot, tedious labor of farming and gardening was rewarded in the season of ripening and harvest. He also taught me how to whittle, hunt quail and rabbits, and most importantly, fish. Nobody loved fishing more than Pappa Jim and me, and there was no place we enjoyed that vocation more than at the lake on Pappa Jim's farm. He even built a special bench near the dam where we could sit under the shade of a towering oak, which he called "Old Bertha." We would sit under that tree and while away the long hot summer, talking and laughing, and eating the sandwiches Grandmama had prepared for us. On occasion, we would catch a mess of fish, which would end up as the main course for the evening's meal. I still remember the first fish I caught—a small crappie. I was only five and couldn't believe my good fortune at catching six fish in quick succession. It wasn't until years later that I found out why I had been such a successful angler. Pappa Jim would distract my attention by showing me the ducks or some other sight while he threw the hooked crappie back into the water for me to reel in once again. I have always felt sorry for that fish. But to a five-year-old, it was magic.

In a way, Pappa Jim was a grandfather to everybody in Ashton. If they needed guidance or advice, he was there for them. Of course, Grandmama didn't call him Pappa Jim. She called him Jimmy, which never sounded right to me. And his three life-long friends, Vernon, Max, and Clarence, with whom he hunted, fished, and on the first and second Friday of each month, played poker, didn't call him Pappa Jim. Vernon called him Jimbo, Max called him Big Jim, and Clarence referred to him as "J." I always found it interesting that he and I were both named Jim, yet nobody called us by our real names.

I guess you could say Pappa Jim was as close to perfect as Grandfathers go. As far as I could tell, he only had one real flaw that stood out: he would not let anyone open a door for him nor would he open the door for anyone else. His peccadillo even extended to my Grandmama. His daughters, including my mother, used to occasionally chide him regarding his peculiar habit. But as always, Grandmama simply laughed and offered everyone a piece of cake, pie, or whatever edible she had handy. When questioned about his conduct, Pappa Jim would typically respond with a shrug of his shoulders or a grunt of indifference. When confronted by his youngest daughter, Aunt Sue, on the occasion of entering the front door of the First Methodist Church for his and Grandmama's fiftieth wedding anniversary, he uncharacteristically bellowed, "Why don't you mind your own damned business?" After that, no one, not even Aunt Sue, ever mentioned it again.

In June of 1991, I had my fourteenth birthday. In July, Pappa Jim turned 78. The week following his birthday found us sitting under the cool shade of Old Bertha, sipping Grandmama's sweet tea and fishing for catfish. Following her bout with cancer, Grandmama didn't cook as much as she used to, but she still had plenty of sugar cookies, cakes and pies, compliments of the local Piggly Wiggly.

It was one of those hot, humid, hazy summer afternoons. Pappa Jim and me weren't sure whether we wanted to fish or take a nap under Old Bertha's protective shade. When he finished the last of his tea, Pappa Jim wiped his khaki shirtsleeve across his mouth.

"Jamie, you're fourteen. Caught between childhood and manhood. You got any questions your old Pappa Jim might need to give an answer to? Like the birds and the bees? You know those girly magazines like the one your old Grandmama found under your mattress last Saturday morning don't necessarily give you the real low down."

I said nothing and looked down at my feet, gingerly holding my reel and rod. I didn't have to say anything. My beet-red face said it all.

Suddenly, Pappa Jim roared with laughter and slapped his right knee. "Boy, don't worry about it. It's natural to be curious at your age. You know where to find me if you want to talk about it."

Pappa Jim leaned back against the trunk of the old oak tree and pulled the bill of his fishing cap down over his eyes.

"Pappa Jim, I do have one question."

After a few moments, Pappa Jim raised the bill of his cap and looked at me. "Well Jamie, what is it? What's on your mind?"

"Why don't you let people open doors for you and why don't you open the door for Grandmama?"

Still reclining against Old Bertha, Pappa Jim looked at me for a long time before responding. When he did, he had a far-away look in his eyes, a look that made me wish I could take the question back. It was as though he was looking at something in the distance that I couldn't see.

"Jamie, meet me at the house day after tomorrow after you get home from school. I'm going to show you something. You're fourteen now. Maybe it'll do you some good. Only thing I ask is that you not tell anyone else until after I'm gone."

Wide-eyed at the prospect of our shared secret, I quickly agreed. I slept little that night, trying to imagine what the secret might be. At the appointed time, I bounded up the steps to my Grandparent's house.

"Pappa Jim," I shouted. Grandmama spoke from the kitchen, "Jimmy's waiting for you in his truck."

We rode in silence for a few miles before we turned into an old, ill-kept graveyard on the edge of town. I followed Pappa Jim's quick pace to the back left corner of the cemetery. He stopped in front of three small gravestones, kneeled down and began pulling up the few weeds that had sprung up around the well-kept area. When he finished, he spread a small bouquet of fresh cut flowers in front of the three headstones. The names were barely legible.

"You know who these three fellows were?" Pappa Jim asked, rising to his feet and dusting off his pants.

I shook my head no.

"Their names are Ben Smith, Eli Johnson and Johnny Smith. Ring any bells?" Pappa Jim continued, looking quietly at the headstones.

"No, Sir."

"They were the three black boys who were hung by a mob in the fall of 1933 for raping a young white girl."

Pappa Jim turned and looked at me, his eyes soft and somber. "They were hung by a mob for something they didn't do. The girl's boyfriend cooked up the whole story, and she went along with it. That story ended up getting three innocent boys killed. 'Course, nobody around these parts likes to talk much about what happened."

"That's a really terrible thing, but what has it got to do with you?"

Continuing to look at me with a sadness I had never seen in him before, Pappa Jim fished an old, faded newspaper clipping out of his shirt pocket and handed it to me. I took it from him and read it carefully. The title of the article declared in bold print: "Three Negro Rapists Receive Their Just Rewards!"

"Like I said before, Pappa Jim, it was a terrible thing, but I still don't see what it has to do with you?"

"Look closely at the photograph Jamie. What do you see?"

I studied the faded picture as closely as I could. "I see a mob pushing three young black men out of the jail into the street."

"See the young man holding the jail door open?"

"Yessir."

Pappa Jim sighed, "That young man is me."

Not knowing what else to do, I handed the faded clipping back to him. He carefully folded it before returning it to his pocket. We stood in silence for a long time.

"Pappa Jim, I know you feel bad about what happened, but that was a long time ago. You were barely a man. And besides, you didn't hang those boys; you just held the door open."

Pappa Jim looked at me, his eyes flashing with pain and anger. "I was a damn fool and more importantly, I was old enough to know better."

"But Pappa Jim, you didn't hang anybody!"

"No Jamie, I didn't hang anybody, I just held the door open for the ones who did. I opened a door that I should've kept closed."

"But Pappa Jim . . ."

"No buts about it, I was a part of that heartless, murdering mob. I came to my senses when I saw them stringing those boys up in the town square. But even then, I remained silent. Those three boys, Ben, Eli and Johnny, were only 15 or 16 years old. They had Mamas and Papas and dreams, just like me and you."

Pappa Jim's voice began to crack as his eyes filled with tears. I had never seen my grandfather cry.

"There's not a day goes by that I haven't thought about those three boys and my part in their death. Ben proclaimed his innocence once or twice and then became silent as they placed the noose around his neck. But you could see the anger and hurt in his eyes as he looked out on that hate-filled crowd for the last time. Eli just closed his eyes and sang some kind of spiritual song until the life was choked out of him. Poor Johnny was the youngest and the most pitiful. He messed on himself and called for his mama while the crowd laughed at him. After it was over, I cried all the way home and I've cried many a tear since. But the truth is, I was a part of that 'terrible thing' as you call it. My mama was so disappointed when she saw my picture in the paper that she didn't speak to me for a long time. She and I both knew she had raised me better than that. Fact is the only honorable man in Ashton on that dark day was Arthur Johannsen. He ran a local funeral parlor and was the only person who would take the bodies. During that time, this cemetery was for whites only, but Johannsen bought the plots himself and gave the three boys a proper burial even though it upset some of the locals. To this day, it's understood by all the black folks in Ashton that when one of them dies, they take their business to Johannsen Funeral Home. I come up here every year on the anniversary of the lynching and talk to Ben, Eli and Johnny."

Pappa Jim dropped to one knee and bowed his head. Standing next to him, I bowed my head as well. After several minutes of silence, Pappa Jim rose to his feet and walked slowly to his truck.

We rode back to the farm, neither of us speaking a word. When we pulled up to the farmhouse, Pappa Jim turned off the ignition. He turned to me with a sad smile and patted me on the knee. "So, you see, Jamie, your Pappa Jim's not the man you thought he was."

From somewhere deep within, I felt the tears rising inside me. Wiping my eyes, I looked at my Grandfather, not sure what to say before blurting out, "Everyone makes mistakes."

"That's right, Jamie. But if I'm going to be real to you, you got to know me for who I am—warts and all. Lord knows I have my faults, chief among them the terrible suffering Ben, Eli, and Johnny went through that I played a part in. For our bond to be strong, you and me have to be straight with each other. It's important that you learn something from my mistakes. Maybe some small good can come from the bad that I've been a part of. I know I've put a lot on you this afternoon. I'd be lying if I didn't tell you that in a way, it feels good to let you in on my secret—to maybe let you help me carry my burden in some small way. If this afternoon means anything, I need to know what you've learned from what I've told and shown you."

Pappa Jim waited patiently while I pondered what he said.

"I guess I learned a couple of things," I answered. "What appears to be isn't necessarily so. Nobody's perfect, even the ones you love. And if you love someone, you love them even if they've done something bad. Sometimes we have to carry the bad because we can't make it right. We still have to try—to do the best we can even when it doesn't feel like enough."

I took a deep breath and looked into Pappa Jim's eyes. He said nothing, but his eyes were full of love and compassion. They looked like they were a thousand years old.Now I'm thirty-four, married with a wife and two children. It's been twenty years since that afternoon and ten years since Pappa Jim passed on, but I often think about our days together.

Last night I dreamed I was fishing under the shade of Old Bertha with four elderly black men. They were talking mostly among themselves. As I rose to leave, one of them turned to me with a twinkle in his eye and said, "Jamie, have you caught any crappie lately?"

12   *Midnight at the "Healing Touch"*

The neon "Open" sign flickered out as Madge O'Doherty turned to Nadine and Tiffany.

"Tonight was a long one—longer than usual. I could use a drink about now. How about you two?"

Nadine stretched and rubbed the back of her neck. "How about two or three?"

"How about the whole bottle?" Tiffany replied with a laugh.

Looking at the card table set up in the right corner of the waiting room of "The Healing Touch Day Spa", Madge commented to her compatriots, "Looks like the wives left us a nice spread. Chips and dip, a plate of wings, and a baking tin of brownies."

Nadine held up a bottle. "No rot-gut wine tonight. You've moved us up to a fine blue-collar bottle of Yellow Tail."

Madge laughed. "One of the wives left it for us. I think it was Devin's wife, Melissa. Anyway, we earned it. It was a full house tonight."

The three women pulled their chairs around the table, and after pouring the Merlot, settled down to plates of potato chips, French onion dip, barbeque wings, and brownies.

It had, indeed, been a long night. For the last six months, one night a week after the regular workday was finished, Madge, Nadine and Tiffany gave massages to war veterans suffering from PTSD and other assorted ailments.

It started the day Madge overheard two of the wives talking in the checkout line at Food City about how they were at their wit's end with their husbands' drinking, insomnia, nightmares and depression. As it turned out, one of the women, Jenny, was parked next to Madge unloading groceries. After a brief introduction, Madge got to the point: "Jenny, I can't rightly explain what I'm going to offer you, but maybe it has something to do with my best friend's cousin taking his life after he returned from Iraq. I can't say for sure. But listening to you and your friends inside, I got this strange kind of urge that I needed to do something. So, I'm offering to work out an arrangement for you and your friends to bring in your husbands one night a week for a therapeutic massage. Maybe it could help them sleep or feel more relaxed. Maybe not. But I am willing to . . ."

Jenny studied Madge's face, looking for an angle. "We're pretty strapped for cash. How much would it cost?"

"Not the regular rate. Whatever you can afford," Madge replied.

That's how it started. One night a week, 5:30 p.m. 'til whoever showed up was taken care of. After six months, a strange kind of community emerged. While their husbands were getting worked on by Madge, Nadine, and Tiffany, Jenny and her friends formed their own kind of support group. First it was brownies, cookies, pie, and coffee. Within the month coffee was replaced by wine, chips, and dip . . . and a cup of Joe for the drive home. Jenny always made sure there was food and wine left for the "Healing Touch" team to unwind with after they left.

At first, most of the husbands were reluctant to participate and one, Missy's, dropped out after the second session. And there was Mary Lou's fiancée, Ted, who was banished for pointing to his apparent erection under the sheet and saying to Tiffany, "Why don't you massage that?" The rest of the men settled into the routine, receiving deep tissue, trigger point, shiatsu, and Swedish massages while Jenny and the girls caught up with each other in the lounge.

Nadine refilled her tumbler with Merlot. "Girls, this has been quite a ride. Sometimes I can't tell whether I'm a massage therapist, a counselor, or a priest."

Dipping a kettle chip into the French onion dip, Madge smiled. "Sometimes we're all three."

Tiffany nibbled on a brownie. "Tonight, Teri's husband, Bert, started sobbing. He apologized, but I told him it was okay— that shiatsu often resulted in clients' crying."

"Of course, that's not exactly true," Madge replied, reaching for another chip.

Nadine turned up her wine glass and smacked her lips. "So what? We're just getting a taste of what these guys have been through, and it can get more than a little dark. We're massage therapists, not psychotherapists. I once took a class at the community college that taught us there is a fine line between mind and body."

"Maybe we're a little psychotherapist and a whole lot massage therapist," Tiffany added.

"Or maybe we're more like "pyscho-massage therapists," Nadine chimed in.

Madge raised her glass. "I'll drink to that—the three 'pyscho-massage therapists.'"

The three women raised their glasses and drank.

Nadine lit a cigarette. "You know I'm mighty young to be a grandmother. "

"Not that young," Madge added with a chuckle.

"I'm glad to help, but these boys are getting to me," Nadine continued. "I've even started smoking again. Ralph and Jewel didn't show up this week, but last week he told me about how when he was a Tank Commander in Iraq and went through villages they had overrun, there would be dead and burned bodies lying in the streets."

Tiffany put down her half-eaten brownie. "Don't they train them for that sort of thing?"

Nadine blew a smoke ring. "I'm sure they do, but I guess such things can still get to you. Ralph told me about the same nightmare he keeps having. He rounds a corner in a village they have just taken and there are the heads of three dead children lying in the street—looking at him. It's just their heads, but their eyes are blinking and their lips are moving. He's not sure, but he thinks they are whispering, 'Why?'"

Stubbing out her cigarette, she looked at Madge and Tiffany, and shook her head. "Sweat broke out on his forehead and his right hand began to tremble. I had him get back on the table and worked on him for another thirty minutes in order to calm him down."

"And there was poor Jerry who lost both his legs," Tiffany said, looking down at her hands. "He told me there were days he woke up and could still feel them . . . until he looked down and saw they were gone. He never cried out loud, but I could see him wipe his eyes when he didn't think I was looking. The last thing he said to me before he and Priscilla moved in with her parents in Louisiana, was that he never imagined not being able to do for himself."

The three women grew quiet.

Finally, Madge broke the silence. "I haven't mentioned it to you two, but I worked Jenny in for a session last week while Ned was at work. They are having a pretty rough time of it."

Madge poured the three of them the last of the Merlot.

Nadine lit another cigarette. "Tell Jenny next week she needs to bring a bigger bottle of vino—better yet, Jack Daniels. If we're going to work on their guys until midnight, we're gonna need more incentive, 'cause we're definitely not getting any overtime pay."

"Not even minimum wage," Tiffany added.

Madge looked at her two friends. "I don't say it often enough, but I couldn't do this without you two. I know when all's said and done, working on these men doesn't amount to much more than gas money."

"I . . ." she started to continue.

Nadine interrupted her in mid-sentence. "Good Lord, Madge. You know we aren't doing this for the money. We're doing it for these veterans and their poor wives and children. We can damn well sacrifice one night a week after what they and their families have been through."

"I know, I know," Madge responded.

Folding her hands in her lap, Tiffany spoke up. "I'm here for my cousin, Jarvis, who didn't make it back from the first Iraq war. I can still hear him laugh. He had the best kind of laugh. From down deep in his belly, the kind that could fill a room and make people smile just hearing it."

Once more silence, each woman lost in her thoughts.

Finally, Madge sighed. "Ladies, it's time to turn out the lights. Tonight, this party's over."

Nadine stubbed out her cigarette and massaged her left hand with her right. "I believe these here hands have lost their healing touch. They are all healed out."

Tiffany rose from her chair and began collecting the trash from their night's labor. "Tell you what, Granny. I'll work for you tomorrow so you can rest those hands for the weekend."

"Much appreciated, Tiff. In that case, I'll have a nightcap with ol' Jack when I get home—and I don't mean my husband, Jack."

Madge reached out to Nadine and Tiffany. "Group hug?"

Wrapping their arms around each other, they rocked back and forth and replied in unison, "Group hug."

13 Barefoot Confession

1958 was a year like every other year in the yellow pines of South Georgia. Watching three television channels, attending the Baptist church whenever the doors were open, and attending public schools with no air conditioning with others of your ilk were the sacred routines of community life. I was in my regular spot in Miss Billups' sixth grade class, middle of the last row with a window seat. The trick was that on the first day of class you had to resist the temptation to lag behind with your buddies and be one of the first kids through the door of homeroom. There would always be a couple of other girls and boys ahead of you, but you didn't have to worry. They were the serious students who wanted a front row seat. Their motives were clear enough. They wanted to impress the teacher with their enthusiasm, and a bit of fawning never hurt when it came grade time. Anything less than an "A" would send them into an emotional tailspin so a little apple-polishing, or as me and my best friend, Freddy, referred to it—butt-kissing—provided an extra bit of insurance. Given my "George doesn't live up to his academic potential" reputation resulting from the semi-annual parent-teacher conference and my middling grades, the egg-heads always threw a puzzled look my way as if to say, "Why aren't you lagging behind with the other cretins and misanthropes?" Of course, in their haste to suck up to Miss Billups they didn't understand what the prime real estate in the classroom really was, the three magic desks located next to the windows. I always picked the middle one, close enough to the front to avoid the shenanigans in the last row where the troublemakers and the sullen few resided, and where Miss Billups' eagle eye frequently scanned for any sign of impending doom. But not too close to where she might mistake me for one of the butt-kissers frantically waving their arms to answer the next question before she even finished asking it. Yes, the middle desk next to the window was definitely the "magic seat," the place you could gaze out of the window into the great beyond where your imagination rather than sixth-grade English could take wing. An occasional well-timed glance at the teacher and nod of the head feigning interest about what you weren't paying attention to usually helped maintain a veil of protection that allowed your imagination to sally forth unabated. Of course, my imagination also made room for Miss Billups, our attractive first-year teacher. At eleven I couldn't explain why or how, but I found my eyes strangely drawn to her. Yes, she was pretty, and for several years now there was something about the curve and shape of women that caused me to sit up and take notice. Still, not knowing exactly what to make of such thoughts, or what to do if I did understand them, they only lingered in my young boy's consciousness until the next distraction flew my way. Today was a repetition of all the other days for the last two weeks. Peering out my window, I watched Old Lady Smithwick carrying groceries she bought at the A&P inside the duplex she shared with her cousin, Jake. There were stories about her and Jake, mostly made up from bits of gossip that floated through the ether-sphere of Hahira, the town I called home. Maybe he was her cousin, maybe he wasn't.

Miss Billups cleared her throat. "Class, I want to introduce you to Willie." She cleared her throat again as if something was caught in it. "Willie will be joining our class for the remainder of the term."

All eyes turned to the doorway where Willie Jones stood looking like one of those doomed convicts in a James Cagney movie about to be led to the electric chair. Some classmates stared, others looked away, and the Morgan twins—the first-class assholes that they were—laughed.

Willie just stood there like a broke-down field mule, staring at his dirty, bare feet.

The uncomfortable silence ended when Miss Billups smiled and pointed to a desk in the corner of the back of the room. "There, Willie, you can take that desk."

Columbus had just finished sailing to America when the lunch bell rang. Today's fare was a hard-fried pork chop, string beans, mashed potatoes, and yeast rolls. Lime Jell-O finished things off for those with a sweet tooth. Two bowls containing a square pound of butter also graced each table, a condiment for the freshly baked bread. Freddy and I both came from family traditions of fast eaters. Our mothers toiled in their respective kitchens for several hours preparing meals that they considered reasonably wholesome by the standards of the day. Following the example of our fathers, we devoured the meal she prepared in a matter of minutes, often leaving them to finish their meals alone. Rumor had it that Jenny Phillips' family on Fourth Street lingered over their dinners making small talk and sharing the events of the day with each other. Not so with us. Mealtime was serious business. Other the occasional "pass the cornbread," few words were spoken.

While the other kids attended to their lunches, Freddy and I played "hide the dead fly in the butter." Perhaps, folks in that era were not as hygiene-sensitive, but there always seemed to be a smattering of dead flies on the floor, courtesy of well-timed swats from the kitchen ladies. Retrieving several of the deceased creatures, like novice sculptors, we would carefully bury them an inch or two below the surface of the butter before smoothing away any trace of their new burial ground. Our reward for our diligence was a scream of surprise and horror from classmates who spread a dead fly on their bread, or better yet, noticed a half-eaten fly on what was left of their roll.

While a pork chop was no meatloaf, which was the number one ranked lunchtime delicacy, it served its purpose by providing a bit of nourishment and entertainment before afternoon social studies began. Miss Billups' charges mopped up the remnants of their meal, slurping up their lime Jell-O desserts—all except Willie. Willie sat at the end of his table, two empty seats between him and Nettie Jackson who was known, on occasion, to eat her own boogers. Willie nibbled at the sandwich he had brought wrapped in an old newspaper. He was three dimes short: three dimes—six nickels or 30 pennies— the price of admission to the cafeteria lunch line.

The hour after lunch was the hardest of the day. Drooping eyelids and drowsy brains called for a nap while Miss Billups called for the answer to what was the capital of Argentina. A spitball whizzed by my face when she began to write something on the blackboard. I turned to find Freddy rolling another paper bullet. Two rows behind Freddy in the corner sat Willie, eyes closed and tapping his bare feet, keeping time to some secret melody that only he could hear, a silent tune that helped get him through the day.

I didn't notice that Freddy's next spitball had also missed its mark, demonstrating why Freddy never got to pitch in the neighborhood summer baseball games. Instead, for some strange reason, I found myself looking out of the corner of my eye at Willie's dirty, bare feet. In interrupting the symmetry of the classroom, the order of what was familiar and predictable, I found myself unable to return to the freedom my desk-side window offered me. Twenty-five students, fifty feet covered by Keds, saddle oxfords, and Buster Brown lace-ups except for one, one boy with no shoes who sat alone away from the others. The picture didn't fit the pattern I had grown accustomed to.

"Supper's ready!" No dinner bell. Just George's mother's shrill announcement that the evening meal was ready. Come one, come all. Me, my younger brother, and my father, the honorary head of the household, all hustled to the table. Each in his own way had learned not to keep my mother waiting.

Stew beef, carrots, and potatoes with a side of cooked canned asparagus casserole comprised the evening banquet. Although my stomach growled, I found myself longing for the overcooked lunchtime pork chop and some cold mashed potatoes. My mother cooked everything "well done"—ham, beef, and chicken—it didn't matter. Everything was dry to the bone. The only time juicy and meat could be used in the same sentence in the Jenkins household was when my father grilled hamburgers outside.

Well-done meat was one thing, but add hardtack gristle to shoe-leather-tough stew beef and you could chew on the bite you just sawed off for five minutes or more before being able to wash it down with milk. Add a helping of warm, mushy asparagus casserole and you were ready to run and hide. In fact, my younger brother, Elvin, once feigned sickness to dodge the evening meal. After two tablespoons of castor oil administered by our mother, Elvin never used that tactic again, dutifully gnawing on the contents of the plate set before him.

Homework finished, shower taken, and teeth brushed—more or less—I was getting my clothes ready for another school day. Wiping down my black canvas, white rubber-soled Keds, Willie and his bare feet took center stage in my mind's eye once more. I wasn't certain why. After all, I was just a typical eleven-year-old boy. Still, the thought of Willie as the only person in class with no shoes, lingered. I thought to himself, *Nothing wrong with bare feet in general.* Me and Freddy and our pals often went barefoot during long, hot summer vacations. But that was different. Miss Billups' class wasn't summer vacation and being shoeless in it didn't fit the order of the day.

I stuck my head out of my bedroom door. "Hey, Mom."

Mildred Jenkins put down the pan she was drying, walked into her oldest son's bedroom, and crossed her arms. "What in the world are you looking for in the bottom of that filthy closet? You should be in bed. Tomorrow's a school day."

Pulling a pair of white buck Sunday shoes I had outgrown from the closet, I held them up. "Can I give these shoes to a kid at school?"

"Why would you do that?"

"Because he's the only kid in our class that comes to school barefooted."

My mother unfolded her arms and put her hands in her apron pockets. "And that bothers you?"

"Well, yes. I reckon it does."

My mother's expression softened. "Well, that's a good thing. You can put them in the brown paper sack I saved from grocery shopping."

What does a young boy say to someone he doesn't really know at the beginning of recess when he hands him a brown paper bag with a pair of slightly used white bucks in it?

He says, "Here . . . I thought maybe you could use these."

Opening the bag, Willie peered inside.

I mumbled something along the lines of, "I don't know if they will fit, but . . . "

I didn't finish the rest of the sentence because the lost, dull countenance that had previously isolated Willie from everyone he came in contact with was transformed in the blinking of an eye into a different person. It was the first time I had seen Willie smile. Actually, Willie didn't smile, his whole face turned into a spotlight of happiness. He was so excited he almost looked as though he might start dancing. Willie kept saying over and over, "Thank you. Thank you. Thank you."

Although it didn't look that way to me, Willie exclaimed that the shoes fit perfectly.

That was the good news.

The bad news was Willie began following me around at recess. Each morning and afternoon, he would stand aside at a respectful distance watching me and my friends play together.

People talked and I felt the heat. First looks, then whispers, and finally, my circle of friends grew smaller.

Then one day, I turned to Willie and said the fateful words, "Quit following me around."

A simple enough phrase, direct and to the point. When the words tumbled out of my mouth, the spell was broken. What was left of Willie's desperate, hesitant smile vanished and he became invisible once more. I returned to my eleven-year-old world and the friends I was used to, and Willie disappeared.

I was a boy then. Now, sixty years later, I still remember. I once gave a barefoot boy a pair of white buck shoes when what he needed was a friend.

14   *Cinderella's Slipper*

Niles Norris read over his notes as the precariously perched air conditioner in his office window serenaded him with gasps and groans. Niles smiled to himself and looked up from his case file at his noisy companion exhaling what passed for cool air. "Mr. Frigidare, I think you and me both may be on our last legs."

A year away from retirement, he had been a school counselor for more than thirty years, experiencing everything from angry parents and cut-throat politicians to despondent students, including a suicide attempt and three drug overdoses last year, as well as a school shooting in 2010. Niles had survived it all— even the occasional personal threat and the on-again, off-again law-suit brought against him and the principal for helping remove one of their students from an abusive home environment.

Remembering what Ed Lambert told him at last year's high school counselor's conference, he laughed to himself. "Niles, we live and work in the wild west of raging hormones and high-octane testosterone."

Leaning back in his duct-taped office chair, he took a long, deep breath and slowly exhaled. After all was said and done with all the ups and downs, he wouldn't have changed a minute of it. It was all part of a whole, a purpose of sorts that he had given his life to. Looking at his watch, he muttered to himself, "Anna, where are you?" As if on cue, Anna appeared in his doorway.

Anna Stephens was a senior. The daughter of a local probation officer, she was bright, outgoing and popular. She also owned a unique streak of compassion that was unusual for someone her age. He wished more students were like Anna.

Plopping down in the chair across from Niles, Anna dropped her backpack on the floor.

"I'm already exhausted and the day is only half over."

Niles smiled. "You are definitely a busy young lady."

Folding her arms across her chest, Anna looked at her counselor. "You know Agnes Dawson?"

Niles nodded.

"I've done my best to be a friend to her, but I'm finally hitting a wall. I can't get her to connect with anyone else but me."

Anna leaned forward. "I've been sitting with Agnes at lunch since she transferred here at the beginning of the term. Although she gets on my nerves sometimes, I hate to see her sitting by herself. And I hear the snickers from the other girls. I'm guessing she does too. It's like she keeps to herself and says nothing—even when a teacher calls on her in class. But when I sit down at the table, she becomes a chatterbox . . . I can hardly get a word in edge-wise."

Niles shrugged. "Maybe, she has a lot to say. Maybe she has been saving it up for someone who will listen."

Anna shook her head. "Well, Mr. Norris, it does get tiresome. To make matters worse, all she seems to want to do is fantasize about one thing or another—like she is waiting for some kind of prince to ride in on a white horse and carry her off."

"Sounds like the Cinderella story," Niles replied.

"I guess," Anna sighed. "Like she's waiting for a Prince to put some kind of magic slipper on her foot."

Niles looked at Anna for a moment before responding. "Not exactly. Maybe, maybe not."

"Maybe not what?"

"My guess is Agnes isn't really looking for a Prince," he replied. "She's looking for a slipper—something that fits. Every time you eat lunch with her, she gets to wear a magic slipper for the hour you two spend together. Like it or not, I think maybe you're the magic slipper."

Anna's shoulders slumped. "I don't want to be anyone's magic slipper."

Niles looked at Anna. "Then why do it?"

"Like I said, because I don't like seeing her sitting there by herself, left out and alone. It doesn't feel right."

The two of them sat in silence.

Finally, Anna grabbed her backpack and looked at the counselor. "I thought maybe talking to you might make me feel better, that you might have some good advice for me—that would help me not feel so different from most of the other students. But I have to admit you haven't been much help."

Niles looked out his window then back at Anna. "Actually, I do have some words of wisdom for you."

"What are they?"

"Get used to it."

"Get used to it?"

"That's right," Niles continued. "Anna, my dear, you're an old soul with a big heart. The good news is that you are going to make a genuine difference in the lives of others. The bad news is that it's going to hurt sometimes, especially when you come to understand that folks like you are—will always be—in the minority. But there is some more good news: A small group of truthful, committed, and caring people can still make a big difference in the world around them. They are the only ones who ever have."

Anna rose to leave the counselor's office. "Get used to it?"

Walking down the hallway to her next class, she whispered to herself. "Easier said than done."

15   *I'll Be Seeing You*

White curtains billowed in a warm summer breeze—blue sky and blue eyes—that's the first thing Jake remembered when he regained consciousness.

The nametag of the nurse checking his blood pressure read "Mildred Scott."

"You've got pretty eyes, Millie."

The young nurse drew back and arched her eyebrow. "Mr. Starnes, you have decided to return to us. Good morning to you."

"Name's Jake. Nice to meet you . . ."

"Mildred— my name's Mildred," the blue-eyed nurse replied.

Even though his face hurt, Jake smiled anyway. "You're no Mildred. You are definitely a Millie."

Writing down his blood pressure on the medical chart, Mildred cast an amused look at the wounded GI who had suddenly become conscious. "Is that so, Mr. Jake Starnes?"

"Yep," the young GI replied.

The young nurse busied herself checking Jake's wounds. "You want to know why?" Jake persisted.

"Why what?" she replied as she began dressing the wound on his left arm.

"Why you're a Millie and not a Mildred."

Jake groaned in spite of himself when she pulled the bandage off his rib cage. "Why on earth would I be a Millie rather than the Mildred that I am?"

Jake's throat was dry. He took a sip of water from the cup on his bed-side table. "It's in your eyes. They've got a sparkle to them. Nope, Mildred's too prim and proper a name for you. You are definitely a Millie."

Mildred Scott stared at the GI in bed number six. "Mr. Starnes, I can't decide whether you are still not fully conscious or if this is the real you?"

Jake cracked another painful grin as he extended the fingers of his right hand protruding from the cast. "Jake Starnes in the flesh. Pleased to meet you, Millie."

The sea of faces and bandaged bodies that inhabited the convalescent ward painted a picture that only a catastrophe like war could produce. In a sense, the hospital was an oasis— even if temporary— in the midst of war's carnage. The sights and sounds reflected every bit of the fragility of the human condition. Some of the wounded smoked and joked with each other while others chose silence and stared vacantly at nothing in particular. The moans and occasional screams of the more severely wounded provided an absurd contrast to the light banter and bravado of their more ambulatory comrades. This brotherhood of the wounded came from all walks of life, and every man there, whether he spoke it or not, secretly hoped his wounds would win him a lottery ticket home.

Jake rubbed his fingers across the contours of the belt buckle he held in his good hand. After they killed the sniper, the fellows from his platoon had sent Jake the sniper's belt buckle as a kind of trophy along with a note. The note said they were surprised how young the German sniper was—that Hitler must be on his last leg if he was sending boys to fight. Of course, Jake knew as well as they did, that boys from the Hitler Jugend were often more fanatical and dangerous than regular Wehrmacht soldiers. Jake put the belt buckle and note back in the box. A bullet didn't care who pulled the trigger. Still, it sounded like the sniper was about the same age as Bud, Jake's youngest brother back home. Jake lay back on his pillow and thought about the guys in his platoon. He wondered what they were doing.

Jake Starnes and the boys of the 30th Infantry Division didn't go in with the 1st, 29th and 4th Infantry on D-Day. They received their baptism of fire when they relieved the 501st Parachute Regiment and the 101st Airborne on June 15. The battle for St. Lo got serious during the first part of July. He could feel the hair on his neck stand up as he recalled fighting in the hedgerows. It was almost like fighting blind. The hedgerows were thick and massive—the Americans on one side and the Germans on the other. One ambush after another, machine gun and rifle fire, grenades and even hand-to-hand combat were the order of the day. Both sides strained to hear what was happening on the other side of the hedgerows. The snap of a twig, the clanging of a mess kit or the squawk of a radio could unleash a torrent of fire and a fierce attack. Sometimes sounds were misinterpreted and mistakes were made. Sometimes you shot your own. When that happened, bad dreams were certain to follow.

"Time for lunch, Sergeant Jake Starnes."

That simple announcement—"time for lunch"—pushed the fog of his memories back into the shadows. He looked up. The blue-eyed nurse was back.

"Would you like to try for a short walk outside this afternoon?"

Jake poked his fork at the mashed potatoes. "Depends on who I'm walking with."

The young nurse smiled. "I suppose I could assist you if you promise to behave."

"It's a date," Jake replied with a thumbs up.

It was warm outside. With Millie's help, Jake slowly made his way along a gravel walking path. A small, well-tended flower garden reminded Jake that something still bloomed besides war. The two of them found a weatherworn bench outside the canteen entrance. Millie went for coffee and donuts, leaving Jake to rest up from the walk. The sounds of Glenn Miller and Bing Crosby echoed from inside the canteen.

Jake watched Millie sip her coffee and nibble at her donut. "What's it like?"

"What is what like?" Millie replied, brushing crumbs from her lap. "You know—being a nurse."

Millie didn't know why, but although she was naturally shy regarding personal matters, she found Jake's direct, yet friendly manner, disarming. "The hours are long. There are the blackouts. And of course, there are the patients."

Millie took another sip of coffee. "I remember one twenty-four-hour period when I was responsible for nearly 200 wounded patients spread out in buildings over a city block. There was one poor fellow—he was in terrible shape…"

"Worse than me?" Jake interrupted.

A wave of sadness washed over Millie's face. "Yes, much worse than you," she whispered. "As a result of his wounds, he was paralyzed from the neck down."

Jake reached over and gently squeezed Millie's hand.

Millie looked at the turning blades of the ceiling fan on the porch where they were sitting.

"Maybe the most remarkable thing I have observed since being here is how many times a wounded soldier would point out another patient to me and say something like "Take care of him first. He's in worse shape than me."

The two of them sat on the bench listening to the music from the radio inside the canteen. Bing Crosby crooned "I'll be seeing you."

Jake turned to Millie and said matter-of-factly, "That's our song."

"You don't say," Millie replied, looking at her watch.

"Yep, I do say," Jake responded with a chuckle.

Millie rose from the bench. "Well, Mr. Jake Starnes, what I say is that our pleasant diversion is over. It's time for my rounds."

"Our date."

Millie looked at her watch again and bent over to help Jake stand on his crutches. "Our what?"

As he rose to his feet, Jake's cheek brushed against hers as he whispered in her ear, "Our pleasant 'date' is over."

Night came upon most of the men in the ward, including Jake, with a fitful sleep or what passed for it as memories returned to nest in the restless minds of the wounded.

The 30th Infantry was ordered to breach the German's defensive line in "Operation Cobra." Re-supplied and bolstered by new replacements, Jake and his platoon mates waited. The Air Corps bombardment would be followed by 50 battalions of artillery pounding the German positions. When H-Hour came, the 30th would move quickly through the hedgerows and penetrate the primary line of German resistance, creating enough room for General Patton's Third Army to pass through and move quickly toward the Brest Peninsula.

Fifteen minutes before H-Hour, red smoke shells were launched to provide a clear target line for the allied bombers. Problem was, a southern breeze blew the smoke away from the German line toward the 30th Infantry waiting to attack. The result was all hell broke loose. 1500 heavy bombers released their bombs on top of the boys of the 30th Infantry. Almost 200 men were killed or wounded. Since they were held in reserve, Jake's regiment was spared the carnage.

The next day, the same hellish nightmare happened all over again. A southerly breeze pushed the drifting red smoke back on top of the 30th. This time, over 400 men were killed, wounded or missing in action, including a General and Jake Starnes. When the bombing run had passed, Jake attempted to go to the aid of one of his wounded platoon mates. A sniper's bullet tore through his shoulder, dropping him to the ground. The pain from the shrapnel in his right rib-cage and leg and his shattered shoulder reminded him that at least for the moment, he was still alive. Jake remembered thinking just before he lost consciousness that if he didn't have bad luck, he wouldn't have any luck at all.

Bathed in sweat, Jake opened his eyes, expecting to see the dead and dying. Instead, he heard the sound of summer rain and the muted murmur of voices in the ward. He looked at his watch—3 p.m. Tonight, he would meet her at the canteen for lemonade and ice cream. Tomorrow, he would board a Red Cross ship bound for the states where he would have more surgery on his injured leg.

Jake closed his eyes and thought about the last eight weeks. The ghosts of battle often haunted him at night, but in the morning, Millie came and chased the desperate moments away. In the morning, blue-eyed hope appeared announcing the day's possibilities. Jake wondered how he could sail away from what he had found.

Millie and Jake sat on their favorite bench outside the Canteen sipping lemonade on the warm, summer night. The sounds of a local trio played the music of the day: "We'll Meet Again," "Moonlight Serenade," "That Old Black Magic" and "Chattanooga Choo Choo." After a short break, the musicians began playing "I'll Be Seeing You."

Jake turned to Millie. "They're playing our song. Let's dance."

Millie took two quick sips of her lemonade and laughed. "Jake Starnes, have you forgotten that you are still on crutches and your right arm is in a cast?"

Jake struggled to his feet and reaching out his left hand, looked at Millie in a way she hadn't seen before. "It's our song, it's my last night before being shipped back to the states, and it's time to dance."

Taking his hand, Millie kissed him on cheek and put her arms around him. The two of them swayed to the music where they stood, Jake leaning on his crutch and Millie and she resting her head on his chest. When the music stopped, they continued to sway.

"These have been the best eight weeks of my life," Jake whispered in her ear.

Millie snuggled closer to him.

Jake stopped and tilted Millie's chin with his good hand. "Mildred Scott, I aim to come back after this war's over and marry you."

Millie kissed Jake lightly on the lips. "I hope your aim's good because I will be waiting."

Wartime romances born in the heat of uncertainty had a rhythm all their own. Lovers experienced an intensity that was often absent in times of peace. The deliberate pace of courtship was swept aside in the tidal pull of living in the moment when the moment was all you had. Some wartime romances survived and flourished, but most, like Jake and Millie's were lost to distance, duties, and plans for a secure future. That didn't mean the sentiments disappeared or were forgotten. Rather, they were locked away in a small, private chamber of the heart, a place where one could visit from time to time and remember.

Jake married Nancy and Millie married James. Jake and Nancy settled in western North Carolina and raised three daughters while Millie and James ended up in Oklahoma with a son and a daughter. After Nancy died of cancer, Jake puttered around his shop with his best friend, "Mercy", a black lab. He bought a new pick-up truck to celebrate his 80th birthday.

Mildred, who decided after the war that she preferred to be called Millie, received a call from James, Jr. that her husband had died of a massive heart attack while fishing in his beloved bass boat with his son. As he requested, Millie had him buried in his boat with his favorite fishing gear. It took six months for Millie to finish with all the details of living and dying that her life with James represented. Between visits with her daughter Edna and son, James, Jr., and her grandchildren, she began to take an inventory of her life. Old memories and friendships, feelings of gratitude and regret, found their way back into her consciousness.

On a lazy Sunday afternoon, Edna noticed an old photograph album with a bookmark on her mother's bedside table next to the family Bible. Opening the album revealed a picture from another time—a photograph of a smiling young nurse and a GI sitting on a bench holding hands. Edna also discovered a packet of letters in the inside back pocket of the album. Over the next several visits when her mother was working in her vegetable garden, Edna would read one or two of the letters. Finishing the last one, she looked out the window at her mother pruning a rose bush and sighed. Placing the album back in its spot on the table, Edna smiled and waved at her mother.

Jake could see the back of her head. He knew it was her when she took a sip of lemonade—two sips—always two sips—no more, no less. He smiled at Edna and his youngest daughter, Mildred.

The banner across the band's stage read "Senior Center Valentine's Dance." The DJ punched a button and the first strains of "I'll Be Seeing You" began to play. Jake could see her hand holding the lemonade tremble with the song's first notes.

Jake straightened his tie. He never liked them, but tonight he would make an exception. Edna and Mildred watched him limp over to where Millie sat. Bending over, Jake whispered in Millie's ear, "Mildred Scott, may I have this dance?"

Catching her breath, Millie looked at the man standing before her and arched her eyebrow. "Jake Starnes!"

Taking her hand in his, Jake led her to the dance floor. Millie looked at him, her eyes bright with surprise. She kissed him and smiled. "You dancing has improved."

Jake grinned at her. "I've had sixty years to practice."

Millie kissed him again and nuzzled her head against his chest. The Glenn Miller Orchestra played as Jake and Millie danced into the past.

16   *The End Is Near*

From a pigeon's vantage point high atop the Mercantile Bank, the mass of people scurrying along the avenue below looked like the tide of some great ocean. There is a certain rhythm and symmetry to the movement of people going to work. The early morning cadence was quicker and more stiff-legged than the evening quitting time promenade.

Why did they walk that way?

Perhaps their slightly desperate gait was motivated by a fear of being late and the heavy-lidded glances of disapproval that would be sure to follow. Other travelers in the urgent parade may have had a driving desire to be the early bird that gets the worm or at least hold onto the part of the worm they had. The advantage they pursued was driven by a caffeine fortified staccato march toward the day's demands.In the midst of this swirl of humanity stood an old man with a sign. The cardboard attached to a broom handle broadcast the message in large red letters: *Repent! The End is Near!*

The sign bearer was tall and gaunt with a long, meticulously groomed white beard. He wore a faded, red plaid flannel shirt, blue jeans that had seen better days, and white patent leather loafers. Perched on his head was a greasy baseball cap with an American flag pinned one side and a silver cross pinned on the other. His angular face framed deep-set clear blue eyes and wore a somber expression.

The current of men and women swept past him without so much as a glance.

Across the street, three well-dressed men in their thirties sat in a café and sipped the remnants of their Starbucks and observed the old man.

The first man said, "He's got to be crazy—standing in the middle of the business district with that goofy sign. Somebody ought to call the police."

The second man replied, "He may be a little off, but I doubt he's dangerous. He probably just wants some attention." The third man said nothing and continued to sip his coffee.

The first man turned to him. "Bill, what do you think? Is the old man crazy-dangerous or crazy-harmless?"

"Maybe neither."

"Neither," the second man queried. "What kind of answer is that?"

Bill drained the last of his coffee and tossed his cup in the trash can. "Maybe he knows something we don't."

All three men chuckled at the thought of it.

"Maybe. I'll go ask him."

"You've got to be kidding. That old man may pull a knife on you. You know how unpredictable those kinds of people are."

The second man chimed in, "He may even hit you with his sign."

The first and second man laughed, but stopped when they realized Bill was serious.

Bill turned to his two companions. "Did you notice the first word on his sign?"

"You mean 'repent'?" The second man replied.

Bill took a sip of his coffee. "That's the word."

"So what?" interjected the first man.

Bill put his coffee cup down and looked at the two men sitting across from him. "I've been thinking a lot lately about what it is that we do for a living—what it means to work for a hedge fund on Wall Street. We've made a ton of money. Our investors haven't been so fortunate. They've lost a lot of their money—some have lost everything."

The second man looked at the first, then back at Bill. "Welcome to the world of finance. You place your bets and take your chances. You know as well as we do that derivatives are a complex and sophisticated financial instrument. Sometimes it can be hard . . ."

"Cut the bullshit," Bill interrupted. "No matter how you dress it up, it still boils down to the fact that we sold bad debt to good clients whose only mistake was to trust us."

"We did nothing illegal," the first man chimed in. "So, what if we made a lot of money? The guys at the top made a lot more. We explained the terms and risks to our clients. We put it all in writing."

"Explained it my ass," Bill replied. He could feel his face turning red. "How can we explain something we don't even understand. Hell, Albert Einstein couldn't decipher the fine print in our clients' contracts."

The second man shifted uncomfortably in his chair. "Bill, what's gotten into you? We all got record bonuses last year. It's not our fault that the investments went south. We followed the lead of the firm's senior partners. If anyone did, they were the ones that dropped the ball."

Bill drained the last of his coffee and placed his cup on the table. "I'll tell you what's gotten into me. For the most part, it's extinct on Wall Street—it's called a conscience. When I look at that old man's sign across the street, it's easy enough to believe that we have plenty to repent of."

The second man turned to Bill. "Speak for yourself, I'm just doing my job and supporting my family—all legal and above board."

"Maybe legal, but hardly above board," Bill replied with more than a hint of sarcasm.

Bill's companions slid their chairs back and stood up. "Come on Bill, we'll be late for work. It's Friday, you'll feel better after a long weekend."

As the two men crossed the street, they realized Bill had turned toward the old man. "Pardon me, Mister."

The old man turned to the sound of Bill's voice.

"I'd like to know why you are standing here with that sign?"

"What's your name, son?"

"Bill."

"Well, my name's Henry. Nice to meet you, Bill."

"To answer your question, I'm fishing for souls."

"Fishing for souls? What kind of answer is that?"

"It's the only answer I've got. I'm fishing for souls and this here sign is my bait."

Bill rubbed his chin. "So, you don't really believe what your sign says is true?"

"Young friend, I don't believe it to be true, I *know* it to be true."

"How can you know something like that."

"I just do."

"Sounds like a crock to me."

The old man said nothing.

"The sign says repent."

"That's right."

"What am I supposed to repent of?"

"Whatever you need to repent of?"

"That's not much of an answer."

The old man pulled a toothpick out of his shirt pocket and placed it in the corner of his mouth.

"I agree, it's not much of an answer, but it's enough."

"Enough for what?"

"Enough to get you moving to where you need to go."

"Well, Henry, my friends were wrong about you. You're not crazy, but I must say you don't make much sense."

"I'm not here to make sense."

Bill turned to leave, then stopped and looked into the old man's eyes.

"What's the point of repenting if the end is near—if it's all over anyway. What difference does it make?"

"Question is my young friend, what difference does it make to you?"

Bill looked at Henry then at a flock of pigeons swooping toward a high perch across the street. "I guess I'm not sure."

Henry pulled a pack of chewing gum from his shirt pocket and handed a stick to Bill. "Try a piece of Juicy Fruit. It'll put a touch of sweet on the bad taste you're feeling inside you."

Bill popped the gum in his mouth.

Henry reached out and placed a hand on Bill's shoulder. "What's troubling you, son? What sorrows got hold of you?"

Bill stared down at the sidewalk. "I got a decision to make—maybe the biggest of my life." He looked up. "I don't know why I'm telling you—I shouldn't."

Henry gently gave Bill's shoulder a gentle squeeze. "That's your call. Little choices along the path lead each of us to a place where a big decision is headed our way."

"I know," Bill replied, the strain clearly showing in his face. "I've made a lot of money with the firm I work for, some of it questionable. I mean, it's legal according to our corporate attorney, but our investors have gotten hurt—some even ruined—by the products we sold them."

Bill paused, pondering if he should say anything else.

Henry waved at a passerby and turned back to Bill. "Legal don't necessarily make something right. Sometimes it does. Other times, legal covers a lot of darkness and hurt, makes folks feel better about something they should feel bad about."

Bill pulled out a handkerchief and blew his nose. "Yeah, it seems like what's left of my conscience has finally caught up with me. A fellow from the Justice Department wants me to testify against one of our senior partners. They aren't after me, or so they say, but apparently have something on him. They want me to help them—do the right thing and all. Doing the right thing will cost me my job, an income my wife and daughter depend on. That's a hell of a price to pay."

"True enough," Henry replied. "That said, you don't seem too happy with the price you been paying."

"Paying for what?"

Henry flipped his toothpick into the trash can he was leaning on. "Sounds to me like you been paying a right heavy price for your self-respect. What price is that worth—or your soul for that matter? You reckon your family would rather have all of you or just the part you been showing them?"

Bill ran his hand through his hair. "Good question. That's what I noticed about your sign. If I repent and testify, the end is near. It will be over for me. We will have to make some hard changes. Put a lot behind us—friends, standard of living, and God knows what else."

Henry looked at Bill. "You know what you need to do, and God knows what else. Like I said before, it's your call."

Bill offered his hand to Henry. "I thank you for your time. I've got an appointment to keep. My life's about to end as I've known it."

Bill turned to walk away.

"There's one more thing," Henry shouted.

"What's that?" Bill replied, looking back over his shoulder. Henry's blue eyes danced, and the corner of his mouth formed the hint of a smile. "The end is near, but so is the beginning."

About the Author

Michael Braswell has published books on the Spiritual Journey and Ethics as well as two novels and three short-story collections.

His personal website is: michaelcbraswell.com.